me too

Also by Vera and Bill Cleaver

me too

Vera and Bill Cleaver

J. B. Lippincott Company
Philadelphia and New York

U.S. Library of Congress Cataloging in Publication Data

Cleaver, Vera.
  Me too.

  SUMMARY: Hoping to expunge neighborhood prejudice and to do
something everyone else has failed to do, a twelve-year-old desperately
tries to teach her retarded twin.
    [1. Mentally   handicapped—Fiction. 2. Prejudices—Fiction]   I.
Cleaver, Bill, joint author. II. Title.
PZ7.C57926Me   [Fic]   73-7631
  ISBN-0-397-31485-X

to Mell Busbin
and those he enlightens

one

There were four in the Birdsong family, two parents and a pair of girl twins, Lydia and Lorna, twelve years old. This doublet was not identical although strangers would sometimes remark they couldn't tell the difference between them. Each had eyes the color of nickel and they wore their chocolate-colored hair pulled back and up with rubber bands wound around the strands so that it appeared something sprouted from the tops of their heads and they had big, white teeth and shoulder blades like chicken wings and knobby knees. Lornie's walk was peculiar. She went in a queer, limp way with her head pulled down to one side, though there was nothing wrong with it or any part of her physically. Beginning at three o'clock each Sunday afternoon and ending at three o'clock each Friday afternoon she attended a school for exceptional children. This institution was in the town and was about a ten-minute drive from the Birdsongs' house.

On weekends when Lydia and Lornie were together Lydia was the boss and told her sister how to act and do. "Use your napkin, Lornie. Don't eat the toothpaste, it's to brush your teeth with. I don't see how you can be hungry again so soon, you just ate. Don't try to push that stick through your head, Lornie. It won't go because there's stuff between your ears. (I hope. Pray to sweet Jesus.) Wait for the light to turn green, Lornie."

They would walk up and down their street which was named Poe and Lydia would long to be anywhere else but there. Lornie shuffled and never offered anything interesting. She, Lydia, had to scrape around and produce that: "Oh, look at that cloud. Like popcorn. Oh, look at the little bird, isn't he sweet? Oh, look at that fire hydrant, isn't it red? Want me to speak some Italian to you? Okay, listen to this. *Non so, parto, parlo, parli.* You want to know what that means? I'll tell you anyway. I said, I do not know, I leave, I speak, you speak."

And Lornie might manufacture her own foreign language and say, "Shoost."

"Billy Frank Blue and I learned that from a book

his sister's fiancé brought back from Italy," Lydia would say.

With simple conviction Lornie would agree. "Yer." And might add this: "Ther kluk and ther twit." It wasn't an insult or anything like that; that's just the way she talked a lot of the time.

"Look," Lydia might say. "Here comes Mrs. Dragoo. Say hello to Mrs. Dragoo, Lornie. (Fat old turtle. Why does she have to be our neighbor?) Oh, and she has her nice children with her. Say hello to Annabelle and Elzora, Lornie. (What beasts and not a lick of brains between them.)"

Lydia's head was stuffed with brains, her father said. She inherited them from him, he said, and taught her how to use a slide rule and about the stars in the heavens and to perceive the world and people as if she might be looking at them through an imaginary magnifying glass. She inherited his kind of glands and they kept her on the move, made her restless and curious and ambitious. Her father's ambitions for her were many. He demanded that she learn more and more and more until finally, one day when she was eleven, she said to, him, "Oh, stop hounding me, I'm going as fast as I can. I'll be what I can be as soon as I can and not before, so stop pushing." After that their friendship cooled.

On weekdays, after school, she ran around the town with Billy Frank Blue. One time they got the idea to fry and eat some grasshoppers, which tasted like vitamins, and another time found a dead snake and tried to stuff him in a jar of alcohol to preserve him only, to their horror, they found he wasn't dead. He writhed away from them and escaped.

Up until the time of this summer, this memorable summer, Lydia's relationship with her twin was of the kind you might have with a five- or six-year-old kid. He's all right when he's asleep and you wish he'd do it more because when he's awake he's dead baggage, a nuisance and an embarrassment. Lornie was that. One Saturday afternoon when Lydia and Billy Frank had her in tow they went to one of the town's parks and she leaped into one of the pools and had to be fished out, kicking and shrieking. Other visitors to the park came running and Lornie showed them her algae-green-stained pants and a choked goldfish. Another time while Lydia and Lornie waited in a hospital corridor for their mother to get off duty, Lornie pushed a fire button and all Lydia could do was yank her into a ladies' room and wait for the excitement to be over. Their mother, Muzz, said, "Well, she didn't know." That is how she always excused Lornie.

Long ago their father had stopped being concerned with the things Lornie did or caused. Now in a strange, frugal way he only observed them or listened to them being told. Old angers once caused by Lornie could not be stirred in him and new ones could not be kindled. On weekends when Lornie was home from her school he did the yard work, washed the car, and read stacks of books.

Lydia thought the kind of life she and her family

had then would last forever, but one Sunday night in the summer when she and Lornie were twelve it came to an end. During the evening meal the parents were cold and sharp with each other and after it Muzz dressed and went out alone. At ten Lydia went to bed but in one of the postmidnight hours she was awakened by some sound or some feeling in the house that didn't belong. She went from her bed to the room her parents shared, knocked, and when there was no answer, edged the door open and looked in. Nobody was there. She went through the house looking. It was dark and quiet, the brownness of the night hovering close to it. On the patio beyond the coolness of the bay windows and glassed doors fireflies winked among the ornamental greenery. She went back to her room and sat on the edge of her bed in the darkness licking her front teeth.

She sat waiting, waiting, though what she was waiting for she didn't know. In a minute she got up and went to her window and looked out. The lawn shone darkly with the dew. The metal linkings and posts of the fence separating lawn from street looked wet.

Lydia saw her father going across the lawn. He carried something with a handle and he wore a business suit. As she watched he reached the gate, unlatched it, and stepped through. He locked the gate behind him, turned, and started off down the street, walking the way Lornie walked when she was being stubborn, running away from something wrong she had done.

Lydia stood by her open window and watched her father go away from home. She didn't know he was going for good, she couldn't. Yet her head began to tremble and her heart turned and inside herself she felt a warning. She put her hands on the sill of her window and called through the screen, "Dad! Dad!" And then, in this moment of unnamed panic, she pushed at the screen with all of her strength. It didn't give because it was secured fast in its frame. It wasn't any good the way she struggled with the screen; it didn't make any sense yet she couldn't stop herself from doing it. It was as if someone else was doing this senseless, silly thing and she was bearing witness to it. And watching, all the while, the figure of her father melting into the brown street shades, disappearing. She heard her breath coming and going. There was pain in her throat and in her temples. The panic in her turned to terror and gave a surge. It snapped her breath. She heard some cats howling. A spidery piece of lightning licked the brown sky. It didn't make any sense, none of it did. And it wasn't any good, not any of it.

two

At once there began the necessity of fitting in and settling to this newer set of circumstances and this was like taking a jigsaw puzzle with some of its important pieces missing and trying to fit it together to make a complete picture. Completeness in anything was important to Lydia. Holes in puzzles bothered her and she would not fill them with makeshift. Even the messages she wrote to herself had to be correct and finished. Crossed-out words and messily formed letters were inexcusable and unforgivable.

On the day of the morning after her father left

home she wrote a message to herself: *Nobody ever said love was easy*. After she had written it she sat staring at the scrap of paper, dismayed. It was queer and crazy. She couldn't remember ever having had a thought like that but she must have had, else how could she have written it? Squinting and scowling, Lydia considered. Oh. That thought was one of her mother's. Lydia closed her eyes and remembered her mother's voice, silken and smooth as water, defending Lornie to her father: "Well, Gordon, nobody ever said love was easy."

He didn't like us, thought Lydia, let alone love us. Especially Lornie. She tore the first message up and wrote another: *Let any man who doesn't honor and love his little child, even if she's exceptional, go straight to hell*. Ah. What magnificent desolation there was in this.

She said to her mother, "I think we should phone the police. Sometimes people get sick all of a sudden and they run away from home because they don't know what they're doing."

"He knew what he was doing," said Muzz. "He's always known. Your father was unhappy here with us. He's been unhappy here for a long time and he's wanted to go and now he has."

"Why didn't you tell me?" asked Lydia because she couldn't think of a thing else to say. It was pretty shrewd and brainy the way she and her mother sat there calmly talking about the situation. Anybody else would have been throwing fireball fits. There was this much to be said in favor of the rotten, stinking mess. It proved hearts don't break. The heart is an organ that pumps blood and that's all.

Though it was forbidden and she didn't like the taste of it especially, Lydia poured herself a cup of coffee and added three heaping teaspoons of sugar to it. She thought about Lornie who loved coffee, in fact anything to eat or drink. When Lornie ate or drank she drooled and did a lot of messing and that was one of the things that had so disgusted their father.

Poor Father, thought Lydia, and raised her cup of steaming brew to her mouth, blew her breath into the brown liquid and let a little puff of steam out. She inhaled it which almost made her cough. And then in anger she thought, he is my father and Lornie's but he never knew us. All he ever wanted from us was learning and to win. He actually expected Lornie to win that time she had a fight with Elzora Dragoo. Lornie will never win a fight with anybody because she can't think quick enough. I know that. Why didn't he? Lydia sat still in her chair sipping her coffee and in between sips licked her big front teeth.

Her mother was saying, "Lyddy, I couldn't tell you your father was unhappy here with us. You're only twelve."

Up until last night I was twelve, thought Lydia. Now I'm sixty-two. Aloud she said, "Well, where do you think he'll go?"

"I don't know," replied Muzz. "His letter said he didn't know where he was going. He said he'd write."

"He didn't take all his clothes. That might mean he means to come back pretty soon."

"I don't think so," said Muzz. "I'm not planning on it."

"What about money?"

"Well, I'm working and naturally I'll go on working. I'm off this morning but only because of this mess."

Lydia held herself steady. This was no time to let excitement show. There was pain between her shoulder blades and a tic in her right cheek. She held her neck stiff and tried to think of the problems. Money had always been one and now no doubt it would be bigger than ever. She said, "Well, all right. It looks to me like he could've given us some notice but he didn't so I don't care. I think I'll go out and get myself a job. Maybe I could deliver papers or set me up a shoeshine stand downtown. Lornie has to be kept in her school and that takes lots of money. There's no sense in me just sitting around here all summer by myself on my royal. School's out."

Lydia's mother said, "Lyddy, I've decided to take Lornie out of her school for a while."

"Oh," said Lydia. "Well, that's amazing. When?"

"I thought today. I thought I'd call now and make the arrangements and then go after her about noon."

"You need me to go with you?"

"Not really."

Lydia said, "Okay, I'll be here when you get back but right now I'm going to run over and see Billy

Frank for a minute. He's got some seahorses ordered for his aquarium and they might get here today. I told him I'd help with them." She wanted to go and sit on the railroad trestle and play her harmonica. Maybe this time when the freight train came slithering 'round the bend she wouldn't jump at the last minute but throw herself beneath its wheels. *WHOOOEEE! WHOOOEEE!* The engineer wouldn't be able to slap on his brakes in time. What a stink there would be. Her father would have to come back for the funeral and people would say, "Well, what'd you expect, fool? For her to dance a jig when you left? She was a normal kid and this is one of the things normal kids do when their fathers desert them. Don't expect any sympathy from me because I haven't got any to give you."

Lydia's mother was clearing away their breakfast dishes from the table. "What do you think, Lyddy? Do you think you and Lornie can get along all right by yourselves while I work? Just for the summer?"

"Certainly," replied Lydia. She thought, Hooboy, that'll be something. She went out and stood in front of her house for a long time watching the street and thinking about the stuff of life. The sun was a powerful presence, yet when she leaned against the gate and closed her eyes she felt no warmth, only a cool, washed vacancy. The image of her father going away from home would forever be imposed upon her mind. Her brain was like a ball of glass. She could see through it, clear to its innermost workings. Its colors were hard and pure and, turning her gaze inward to it, she saw her father go over its brown horizon and then Lornie appeared, walking in that queer, limp way she had, intently chewing her nails, her nickel-colored eyes a little sly, depthless. Such a sad little bird. A monkey. A butterfly without wings.

Nervousness began to buzz around inside her. Lornie could be endured for weekends but a whole summer of her was unthinkable. She did so much messing and you didn't dare leave her alone for five minutes and when you told her to do things you had to remember also to tell her when to stop. She couldn't be trusted alone on the railroad trestle. What if, sometime, she wasn't told to jump? And people pitied her and were suspicious of her.

Lydia took her harmonica from her pocket and raised it to her mouth. She tooted three loud, wild notes and it pleased her to see the response from the house across the street. Mrs. Dragoo popped out of its front door and flapped down its front steps, rolling her eyes and squawking. "Lydia!"

"Ma'am?"

"Stop that infernal racket! You know Elzora and Annabelle always sleep late!"

Lydia went to her gate and loosened its lock-catch but did not do this with her hand. She did it with her bare foot, hooking her big toe under the lock in an elaborate manipulation which had taken her days to perfect. She licked her big front teeth and turned her head violently from side to side. She grinned and out of the corner of her eye watched Mrs. Dragoo who had come as far as the curbing on her side of the street. Loud enough for the neighbor to hear, Lydia spoke to her toe. "Well, fool, you going to open the gate or not? Come on, you can do it. I showed you how, don't you remember? Oops, watch out, fool! Nmmmmmmmpht! Phfffffft! Ah, there you are! See, I told you you could do it! Good girl, Pinky! Good girl!" Lydia stood on the street side of the gate and grinned at Mrs. Dragoo. She said, "There now, Mrs. Dragoo, how about that? Wasn't I amazing?"

The fingers of one of Mrs. Dragoo's hands lay out-spread on one of her cheeks. She made no reply. When she turned to a bush to pluck her morning paper from its branches, Lydia was struck anew with her judgments of this woman. Mrs. Dragoo was the kind who had a mistrust of anything irregular and her two creepy children were the same. Their brains were locked in cages. Annabelle Dragoo thought pasteurized milk was called that because the cows it came from got their food in pastures and Elzora Dragoo wouldn't look at a shooting star and always thought bugs were crawling on her.

Mrs. Dragoo had gone back into her house. The street lay warm and hushed under the sun, the June sun. Lydia crossed it and cut through the Dragoos' side yard. Beyond this there was a long, sloping stretch of tree-studded property belonging to the town, and after that a little, unshaded, forlorn store surrounded by sand and blackberry briar. And after that some more trees, then the body of water she had named Froggy Pond. It was shaped like a saucer with a neck that fanned out into a pool beneath the railroad trestle.

Lydia sat on the trestle and played her harmonica. Beneath her dangling feet the amber-colored water was alive with light: green around the edges with loosestrife and spider lilies. The sun was climbing and the music she persuaded from the harmonica was too lonesome. She stopped playing and knelt between the tracks with her ear to one of the rails. Not a sound. The train was still too far away, an hour at least. She sat again with her legs crossed, Turkish fashion, and her eyes squeezed shut. She thought about Lornie and her father and in a minute opened her eyes and dug into her pocket for a stub of pencil and one of the little squares of paper she was never without. On her updrawn knee she wrote a message to herself: *I say love is not easy. It's sesquipe-dalian. That means a foot and a half long.* Temporarily that satisfied her. She played her harmonica all the way back to her own neighborhood, to Billy Frank Blue's house.

Billy Frank looked quite a bit like an Eskimo, especially when it was winter and he trotted back and forth to school bundled in a parka with a thick hood that tied under his chin. His patent leather bangs were straight across on his forehead and his black teddy-bear eyes never missed a trick, he was in such a hurry to know everything and do it all. He realized his likeness to Eskimos and whenever the spirit struck him he talked about going to the Arctic to live. When he was eighteen, he said, or twenty. Somewhere about in there. Meanwhile he was twelve and stuck with being a southern American, and a set of average parents, both employed in the offices of a soft-drink company, and an older sister named Rucelle.

Rucelle was eighteen and engaged to marry a seagoing sailor named Harley Bell. To Lydia she appeared a wasted girl, spending all of her days writing letters to Harley Bell and waiting for his replies. She was friends with the Dragoos. At least once a week she suppered with them and never paid admission when she went to see movies at the Queen Theater, for Mr. Dragoo was its manager. Whenever he and Mrs. Dragoo wanted some time away from their children Rucelle went over and stayed with them. According to Rucelle, Annabelle and Elzora Dragoo had never done a wrong or ugly thing and never were going to. They were such bright and lovely-mannered children. Rucelle always said she loved them, enlarging her pale, frozen eyes to let you know the honesty of this feeling.

On this morning when Lydia knocked on the Blues' back door Rucelle opened it. She was dressed to go out and smelled of coffee and sleep. "Oh." she said. "It's you. Why don't you ever use the front door like other civilized people? Were you raised in a barn?"

"No," answered Lydia. "Where's Billy Frank?"

Rucelle enlarged her pale, frozen eyes. "How should I know?"

"If I had a brother," said Lydia, "and it was only nine thirty in the morning, I'd know where he was.

Probably he's gone to the express office or the post office to pick up his seahorses. They're supposed to come today. Should I come in or should I just wait out here?"

"Oh, all right," said Rucelle and let her hand fall away from the door. There was a new framed picture of Harley Bell, her sailor fiancé, standing on top of the refrigerator. Knowing Rucelle was ravenous to marry him and feeling a little sorry for her because she was shaped too much like a peanut and Harley Bell was so far away in the Pacific Ocean somewhere, Lydia said, "Oh, I see you've got a new picture of Harley Bell. Isn't he pretty? Don't you hope all your children will look like him?"

Rucelle stood at the table finishing a doughnut and a cup of coffee. In her foggy voice she said, "They will. Why shouldn't they?"

Without being invited, Lydia sat in a chair with her hands folded in her lap. Rucelle always asked that kind of question of anything you could think to mention to her. If you should say to her, "Rucelle, there are some rivers that flow west and some that flow east," she'd say, "Well, why shouldn't they?" Without knowing the answer herself. She was that kind of person.

In a minute Rucelle would go wherever it was she was going and then maybe Billy Frank would come. He might have the seahorses with him and that would be an interesting relief. Lydia stealthily pressed gentle fingers to her temples. They still ached from the night before.

"Harley's intelligent," said Rucelle, holding her empty coffee cup upside down over the sink.

Lydia pushed her back hard against the back of her chair and waited for further revelation. A quiet reasoning voice told her to be silent but she said, "Yes, I know he is."

"You can't know that," said Rucelle, turning so that she faced Lydia. "You shouldn't say you know things when you don't. But I am just telling you. There's never been any insanity or freaks in Harley's family or mine. Nothing like that on either side so naturally our children will be intelligent. Normal."

"I hope so," said Lydia. Rucelle was getting ready to spring some kind of nasty little surprise. Now the expression on her face was too delicate. It tiptoed through her eyes—which really were beautiful, except when you looked in them it was like looking into two glass marbles. The little streaks and wisps in them were milky. It was impossible to see if anything, any meaning at all, lay in back of them. Because of her valuable friendship with Billy Frank to protect, Lydia had always felt the need to pretend, but now, because of what was happening, it seemed a little tiresome to keep on with that. I will handle this, she thought, and a feeling of excitement went up and down through the fluids in her spine.

Rucelle was watering a small pot of cactus that

stood on the windowsill above the sink. She said, "Lydia, I've been meaning to talk to you about something and I guess now is as good a time as any. My parents wanted me to have a little talk with you about my brother."

"We're friends," said Lydia. Rucelle was giving the cactus way too much water. The plant wasn't all that thirsty, not two glassfuls. The water was spilling over the rim of the pot and running down its sides. Lydia said, "Cactus don't like a lot of water. It rots their roots."

"Lydia," said Rucelle. "My parents and I have decided it's not healthy for you and Billy Frank to be such good friends. You know what I mean?"

"No," replied Lydia, deliberately blank and friendly. It was even nastier than she had thought it would be. Why couldn't people let the nice things alone?

"I think you do," said Rucelle and fixed her eyes on Lydia in a dead, still stare. "You're a smart little girl."

"Sometimes I'm smart," said Lydia. "Sometimes I'm not."

"When my parents were thirteen they decided to get married," said Rucelle. "Of course they didn't, not till they were much older, but they never forgot. My dad and his family moved away and my mother and her family moved away but that didn't make any difference. They started to love each other when they were only children and they never forgot. When they were old enough both of them came back here and they got married."

"Well," said Lydia, "when people love each other that's what they should do. Get married. They shouldn't let anything stop them."

"Before two people decide to get married they should know each other," said Rucelle, sharply.

"Yes," agreed Lydia.

"They should think about the children they're going to have."

"Yes."

"By that I mean they should think of their children first and themselves second. For instance, if I was a person with sugar diabetes I'd never get married. That's a disease that can be inherited and it wouldn't be fair to my children so I wouldn't get married and have them. I'd find some other way to live."

The fluids in Lydia's spine had stopped running. The sight of the drowning cactus plant was making her sick. She felt her mind turn and from some hidden spring in it there came streaming a vast feeling of pity for Rucelle and, at the same time, an overwhelming sense of disgust. At length she stood beside her chair gazing at Rucelle with that sad-bright monkey expression so much like Lornie's. There was no use to say, "Rucelle, you could have a child like Lornie. Anybody could. Nobody can tell about their children till they get here. Sometimes you don't know for years; you can't tell. We couldn't tell with Lornie. My mother said not until she was two."

Rucelle was saying, "I'm sorry if I've hurt your feelings." She was using the trick with her eyes, stretching them larger and making them shine with honesty and pure intentions.

"You haven't," said Lydia. "Not one bit." She wanted to run over to Rucelle, leap on her with all fours, and choke her until she was dead. Wanted to grab a butcher knife, cut Rucelle's tongue out, slice it in half, and stuff it in her ears.

Somewhere in the house a clock bell was pealing a little forgotten alarm. It was that which saved Rucelle from being murdered. Rucelle said, "Oh, my goodness, I've got to run." And that was the invitation for Lydia to leave.

She went again to the railroad trestle and sat on it, playing her harmonica. The freight train came and she jumped just in time. The engineer shook an angry fist and then laughed to see that this time she hadn't judged her leap from the trestle to the bank below with enough accuracy. For a minute or so she was in the water of Froggy Pond and when she tried to stand something oozy and strong sucked at her bare feet and legs. The brown water pulled at her. It seemed to brim with some kind of a secret which would remain forever unguessed by her. She kicked at it and it loosened its hold. She lifted her feet and waded in to the bank and sat on it, brushing mud from her clothes and thumping water from her harmonica. Maybe it was ruined.

Annoyed at the tears which drowned her eyes in a stunning, blinding storm, she began to beat the harmonica against her knee and the water drops flew out of its little cells and sparkled where they landed. I am just not smart enough to handle people like Rucelle, she thought, but I have got to get that way. To help myself. And Lornie. To help us all.

With the harmonica she beat on her knee until there was a great, raw bruise, all black and red and purple. It took three wide Band-Aids to cover it.

three

Early in the afternoon of that day Billy Frank wanted to know what the Band-Aids covered and Lydia said, "Oh, just a little old black and blue spot. I get tired of having both my legs the same color all the time so this morning I beat on this one and now it's different. Did your seahorses come?"

"Yes," replied Billy Frank. "I think one of them's pregnant. I can't leave him by himself for very long."

"Him?" said Lydia.

"Yes, him," said Billy Frank, "He's the one pregnant and he's the one going to have babies. That's the way seahorses are. Let's us go over to my house."

Lydia said, "I can't, Billy Frank. Not now. I'm very busy."

Billy Frank gave the impression that he hummed a lonesome tune though no sound came from him. He said, "Well, I'll wait a little bit." And sat on the floor in the doorway alternately cutting his toenails with a pair of nail clippers and reading a book.

They were in one of the Birdsongs' back rooms. She was rearranging it, pushing the twin beds in it closer together, pulling a table to stand nearer the window, delving into a wicker basket for the learning aids once employed by her father to teach Lornie. Books, pencils, crayons, a stack of small printed pictures, sheets with songs and rhymes printed on them, some with missing words. A set of number blocks. All of these things had been only lukewarm successes with Lornie and one by one they had been tossed into the wicker basket. Maybe Lornie would take to them better this time. At least they would keep her hands busy.

In the final days of sitting in this room whenever Lornie was home her reality had become too much for their father. She had never, ever gained any real understanding of anything he tried to teach her. "That is a banana," she would say, pointing to a picture of a bicycle.

And he would shout, "No! No! I just told you it was a bicycle! A bicycle has wheels and you ride it! A banana is to eat! Can't you understand? Can't you?"

Lornie couldn't. Or wouldn't. She would shrug and hop around the room making monkey faces. What difference did it make to her if a banana wasn't a bicycle?

Billy Frank had propped an elbow on the floor and was holding one of his feet in his hand. He had forgotten his toenails and was reading. Whenever he read, a bomb could blow the house around him away and he wouldn't see it or hear it.

Wiping dust from a chest, Lydia said, "Billy Frank, my father left us last night. He's deserted us."

And Billy Frank, settling himself deeper, said, "In a minute. You said you couldn't go just now and I believed you. Now I got to finish this chapter."

"I hope Harley Bell's grandmother is a freak of some kind," said Lydia.

"Shut up," said Billy Frank. "It's your fault I got to finish this so just shut up a minute."

"Is she?"

"No. She's just plain and average."

Disappointed, Lydia sat on the foot of one of the beds surveying the room. It looked nice now. The fat, blue lamp on the bedside stand was just right and the beds so close together made it look homier. Lornie wouldn't notice its changed appearance. She never noticed anything unless you said, "Look." Lydia put her head in her hands and licked her front teeth. A whole summer she would have to spend with Lornie, nursemaiding her, dragging her wherever she herself wanted to go, supervising her eating. Reading to her and telling her stories. And when it was finished nothing would be changed. Nobody could change Lornie; so many had already tried. Their father and mother. The teachers at the school. Even a special tutor one time for three months.

The windows were open and from the house next door, where lived an anonymous renting bachelor, music poured. An orchestra, all the instruments playing together. Lydia left the bed and went to the window and stood with her head cocked, looking at the white and green vinework that splashed the side of the renter's house. Except for the blossoming vine the house was gray and dull and queerly remote. It looked like a little prison or one of those places where crazy people are locked up. How could anybody stand all that racket? The renter must be deafer than a corpse. A rude, creepy old slug. He was the kind of person she saw sometimes in her bad dreams, gliding in and out of them, leering a crinkled blue smile, showing her his trembly white eyes. Whenever the renter was home he played his music and if you didn't like it you could lump it.

Against the side of the renter's grim little house the blooming vine shook its dusty leaves and the music, streaming from the windows, paused. And then began again, swelling, turning, running in a fantastic direction.

Lydia put one hand to her forehead and the other over her heart. As in a trance she closed her eyes, listening, and all of a sudden straining her attention. There was something about the music . . . something. Hitting her, making her mind somersault. A swift, bright streak of identity. Whoever had written that music had her in mind as he created. A little piece of it belonged to her. Was hers. How could that be? It couldn't be, yet it was. How hard to put this thought together.

The voice of the music was the heart of the unknown artist touching hers. She had heard the renter's music before and been irritated by its noise. All that clanging and twanging. How was it she could stand here and think: Now it's beautiful. It's for me. Listen. It's telling me. . . . Ah, the heart must touch the heart. That is its message.

Still with her eyes closed, still facing the windows, Lydia fingered the ends of her hair sprout. Her knee hurt and the roots of her teeth ached. She was excited as she had never been excited. She spoke without turning. "Billy Frank?"

"Just two more paragraphs, Lyddy. I'm hurrying."

"Billy Frank, you hear that music?"

"Yeah, yeah."

"Billy Frank, I know what's wrong."

"Good, good."

"With Lornie, I mean. Why nobody's been able to teach her. I know why now. It's because they've only touched her with their hands. To get to somebody you've got to touch them with your heart."

"Sure," agreed Billy Frank. He hadn't heard a word. In a way this was better because if he had heard he might have laughed and that would have spoiled it.

Lydia's mind began to leap and cartwheel. In ten

seconds it ran down ten roads, returning each time to a big, pulsing intersection. Which way to go, that was the question, and there was nobody to say except herself. The music from the renter's house sounded like a prayer. On lifted wings it spoke to her from an invisible world.

Lydia took her harmonica from the pocket of her shorts and blew a loud, long blast on it. She whirled around in time to see Billy Frank drop both his foot and his book. "I was finished anyway," he said and stood up. He looked a little drunk. "What was that for?"

"For everything," said Lydia. "And everybody. Toot 'em out, that's my motto! Toot 'em out and root 'em out!" She sat again on the foot of one of the beds. The music from the renter's house had stopped.

"I got to go home," said Billy Frank. "You coming with me?"

"No," answered Lydia. "Not today. Maybe not any day ever again. Muzz has gone after Lornie. She's not going to be in her school this summer. I'm going to take care of her all day, every day, while Muzz works. My father has left us, Billy Frank. He's deserted us."

"Oh," said Billy Frank. "Well, that's amazing."

"You don't have to look sorry. I'm not. He'll be sorry himself when he comes back and sees what I've done with Lornie. Things he couldn't do. I'm going to teach her. We're going to sit right here in this room all summer every day and I'm going to teach her and she's going to learn. She can. I know it. Because I'm her

33

other half. For a while before we were born we might've had the same heart. Nobody's ever thought about that. Nobody's ever thought to ask me what I thought. I'm going to show everybody and that goes for Rucelle too, Billy Frank."

Billy Frank blinked his eyes and twitched his shoulders. "Oh, Rucelle."

"Yes, Rucelle. And while we're on the subject of her we'd better get something else straightened up, Billy Frank Blue. I'm never going to marry you."

"What?" said Billy Frank. "What?" The whites of his eyes seemed to disappear into their blackness. His face grew the color of a lime with a peculiar look of pain coming over it. He stepped backward as if retreating from some awesome bodily threat that had been suddenly slung before him.

"I wouldn't marry you if your nose was full of diamonds, and you've got a big one!"

Billy Frank felt of his nose which was a nice size and shaped like a jelly bean. "You're crazy. I never asked you to marry me. I'm only twelve and so are you and I told you a thousand times—"

"Billy Frank, I'm not asking you to marry me. I'm asking you if you ever thought about us in that way, sweet Jesus forbid. Rucelle's the one worried, not me. She's afraid we might get married someday and have children like Lornie. I'm not supposed to go over to your house any more. Wouldn't that kick you around the block, though?"

"I am going to go over to the Dragoos' and kill Rucelle," declared Billy Frank. "She's over there as usual." He was now his natural color. His eyes flashed hot mad. "You wait here. It won't take me but a minute."

"No, Billy Frank."

"What d'you mean, no? She needs killing! It's awful for her to say that! It's worse for her to think it! Nobody knows what kind of kids they're going to have till they get here."

"Yes, nobody."

"She could have been a trick of nature herself. Anybody could. People should think about that once in a while."

"Billy Frank, don't kill Rucelle. Don't even try it. You'd go to jail and I wouldn't have time to go and visit you. Rucelle will get hers. I'll show her. I'll show everybody. By the end of this summer they won't be able to tell the difference between me and Lornie."

The renter had put another record on his machine. This one was all clash and tumult. It made her want to go out on the street and find somebody to pick a fight with. One of the Dragoos. *Halloo, Mrs. Dragoo. How are you? Wahooo. Let's dance. Down to Froggy Pond. Sit on the trestle. Listen for the train. Wahooo. Ewwwww, Mrs. Dragoo. You didn't jump like I told you to. Now look what a mess you've made. I can't hear yooou, Mrs. Dragoo. You're dead.*

While her heart spun with this ambition, seesawing with the mad music, Lydia leaned her head into her hands, staring down at her bad knee. She envisaged how it would be at the end of the summer. One beautiful morning she and Lornie would go out and stand by their gate and Lornie would play the harmonica for the benefit of Mrs. Dragoo who would come flaring out of her house yelling to Lyddy to stop only it wouldn't be Lyddy making the noise. It would be Lornie. Mrs. Dragoo wouldn't be able to tell them apart because Lornie would say good morning without being prompted and she'd be acting like a girl and not like a monkey. She'd smile at Mrs. Dragoo and with her toe unlatch the gate and then Lydia herself would smile at Mrs. Dragoo and unlatch the gate with *her* toe and Mrs. Dragoo would turn white and shriek to Annabelle and Elzora and Mr. Dragoo to come and look and tell her which was Lyddy and which was Lornie. Nobody would be able to tell. It might be Sunday and if it was the church bells would be ringing and at Sunday school Lornie would know her lesson and she'd stand up and recite it. What a joke, what a victory it would be. Their father would hear about it, somebody would write and tell him, and he'd come back. He wouldn't be able to get himself back fast enough to see the miracle. It wouldn't be any of his doings and she'd tell him so. Right to his face. Maybe he'd cry.

Billy Frank had come to stand before her. "Lyddy?"

"I mean it, Billy Frank. Lornie and I are going to sit right here in this room all summer and I'm going to teach her and she's going to learn. I'd thank you not to tell anybody about this. We've been good enough friends for you to do that little favor for me, haven't we?"

"Don't be funny," said Billy Frank. "Lookit, I think I'll go home and get my seahorses and bring them over here. Let's move my whole aquarium over here. It'd be educational for Lornie."

"Billy Frank," said Lydia and could not put a finger on her shame for it wasn't hers. "It's not just Rucelle doesn't want me to be friends with you any more. It's your mama and daddy too. I don't want you in any trouble on my account. Maybe you'd just better go home now and stay there. Maybe you'd better not come over here any more."

All was quiet. Some sun was in the room and the shadow of Billy Frank was cast on the wall, appearing as that of an old bird huddled in an attitude of illness. The renter's music came through the windows and the feeling that bloomed inside her made her feel cheated. "It's not my idea," she said.

Billy Frank almost screamed his retort. "But they can't do this!"

"They're doing it," said Lydia.

"No! No, no! Not to me they don't! I can pick my own friends!"

"They're afraid we might get married someday."

"That's crazy!"

"Of course. But they don't think so." She would leave it to him. If he decided in their favor and against her, well, the world wouldn't blow up. Let everybody desert. More power to them. She wished them luck. God would take care of their miserable hides when the time came and He wouldn't make any bones about it either. He'd send them all to hell where they'd fry eternally. He'd visit His wrath on them, send a horde of blood-sucking mosquitoes to crawl through their screens at night and give them the yellow plague or sleeping sickness. Maybe leprosy. Their fingers and toes would fall off, one by one. Their flesh would fall away and eventually they'd dance around in their bones, their old, miserable, traitor bones. They'd have to go and live by themselves in a leper colony.

Billy Frank towered over her giving the impression of unsuspected strength and sudden growth. "We're friends," he said, "and can't nobody stop us."

Lydia laughed cruelly.

"If they try," threatened Billy Frank, "I'll say I'm going to run away. They're scared spitless of that. Harley Bell's little brother ran away one time and they had to go clear to Las Vegas, Nevada to get him. That's where they do all the gambling and it's a city of sin and Harley Bell's mother almost had a nervous breakdown thinkin' her little boy was ruint for life. He wasn't any more ruint than I am. He told me he lived under a bridge the whole time he was there with some gypsies. I'm going home now for my seahorses. I think I'll move my whole aquarium over here. You decide where we're going to put it while I'm gone. It'll be educational for Lornie."

For the longest time after he had gone Lydia continued to sit, listening to the renter's music. Every once in a while one long, low, clear note in it reached her.

38

four

It would be her mountain and hers alone
for hadn't all the others had their whack at it? Yes, and
they had failed, all the doctors, three or four kinds of
those, the therapists, and the teachers. Even Muzz,
whose love for Lornie was outrageous because it was of
the kind that didn't change anything. It lived to protect
Lornie but not to improve her. It went from Muzz to
Lornie in a blind, unreasoning stream and no one could
say, "You must stop some of this. It is futureless and
you are killing yourself. You aren't doing Lornie any
good either. She must be taught as much as she can be."

Because of Lornie Muzz had migraines and only one friend, a woman named Coochie Pepper. Coochie was married to a man named Tom Ben and it was she who suggested Lornie might be one of God's special children, closer to Him than other people and possessed of some supernatural knowledge and maybe a little power to go along with it.

That would have been nice had it been so but Lydia had done some close investigating and found there wasn't a thing in evidence to support that phantom notion. The rages Lornie sometimes threw were not communications with God or the devil. They were temper fits and what she spoke while beating her heels and throwing herself around was not the language of some disappeared ancient but her own. People were puzzled by her language and some were suspicious of it. She could amaze you by assembling words and speaking them in proper order but usually she preferred her own lingo. Rrrrrrmpht. Whucky koosh? Lala. Nala? Yer, yer, yer.

Lydia imagined Lornie's mind to be laid out in thin little strips no wider than a woman's little finger and smooth—no kinks in them or bulges. Lornie did not experience things, not so you could notice it. She only observed. If she saw a snake swallow a rat she just shrugged. She was not curious. You had to tell her what she wished for: To be a cloud. God for one day. Mrs. Dragoo to produce idiot quintuplets. Mr. Dragoo's theater to burn up. All of the Blues, except Billy

Frank, to be visited by a disease that would turn them to pillars of salt.

To go to sleep all Lornie had to do was find a place. A piece of wall would do, the floor was fine. On this, the day she was taken from her school and brought home to stay, she came from the car into the house, dropped her school satchel just inside the door, looked at the scene of home and said, "Pupple," in the most disgusted way and slammed off down the hallway.

"She's upset," said Muzz. "She didn't want to come home. The teachers at the school were upset. They didn't want to let her go."

"What they want won't make them fat," said Lydia. "They didn't offer to let her stay there for free, did they?"

"No," answered Muzz as if answering a serious question. She gave a push to her blondish brown hair.

"We'll get along all right," said Lydia. "As soon as Lornie gets used to being home all the time."

"Yes, of course we will," said Muzz. "We'll go to the movies. We'll have picnics on Sundays. We'll do lots of things." She jumped up. "But today I still have to go to work. I promised my supervisor I'd come in as soon as I got things settled here. There are some groceries in the car. Would you bring them in?"

The two sacks of groceries and Lornie's one suitcase and three boxes weighed a ton. By the time she got the car unloaded of it all she was sweating. In the newly arranged bedroom Lornie was stretched out

asleep on the throw rug in front of the chest of drawers. Lydia pushed a pillow under her head and Lornie,
without opening her eyes, said, "Whist bird ra ra."

On a lick-and-a-promise bent Muzz bounced
through the rooms pulling the whining vacuum cleaner,
snatching clothes from doorknobs and towels from the
bathroom racks. The washing machine on the back
porch opened its metal mouth to receive them. Said
Muzz, "Can you and Lornie eat out of the refrigerator
tonight? I don't have time to fix you anything. I don't
suppose I'll be home before ten or eleven o'clock."

Lydia said, "Don't worry about us. We won't
starve."

"There's some cold chicken and potato salad. You
could open a can of some kind of vegetable. Oh, and I
bought some fresh cherries. Lornie loves them."

"I'll take care of everything," said Lydia. It was a
good thing she was older in mind than she was in years.
A good thing she was intelligent and had the stuff it
took to handle a situation like this.

The phone was ringing and it was Billy Frank.
There was some commotion in his background and
when Lydia asked what it was he screamed, "I'm at the
dentist's, I said! I forgot I was supposed to get my teeth
looked at today. An old lady just keeled over in here,
they're takin' her out now. Naw, there's nothing
wrong with my teeth but I got to stay here and let the
dentist look at them. I'll be back to your house directly
with the aquarium."

The world, thought Lydia, was just naturally

going to the dogs. She lounged in the doorway of her mother's room, watching Muzz change from house clothes to hospital uniform. "By tomorrow my hours will be back to normal," said Muzz. "I'll be home tonight as soon as I can make it. After it gets dark you and Lornie stay inside. Lock all the doors. Any trouble, you phone me, hear?"

"Won't be any trouble," said Lydia.

The day was aging. She sat on the front porch steps and waited for Billy Frank. She waved her mother good-bye and went to hang the washed clothes on the line in the back yard. On the other side of the board fence the renter's house was silent. He grew his own organic vegetables, didn't trust those from the stores. Every afternoon he brought a stool from his house and sat among the butterbeans and squash and tomatoes transferring ladybugs from a little cardboard carton to the foliage of these plants. They were supposed to keep the plants free of disease.

Lydia finished pinning the last towel to the line and walked over to the fence. In a practiced action she swung herself to its top. It was thin hospitality. The rough wood cut into the backs of her thighs. The renter was sitting in his garden. She called out, "Hiya, Footsie."

The renter's hand which had been delicately transferring a ladybug from its carton to a tomato leaf paused in midair. He looked around at her with a mulish, offended expression. "How are you?" he asked formally.

She almost wanted to laugh for she knew the reason for his sore look. He didn't like her name for him. A dozen times she had asked him to tell her his real one but he wouldn't so she called him Footsie. No reason. Not because he had big feet; actually they were small and too graceful for a man but she had to call him something. Therefore, Footsie.

Conversation with this one wasn't easy. He never volunteered anything. She said to him, "Guess what?"

"I don't want to," said Footsie. "I'm busy. Can't you see that?"

"My sister's home from her school and I'm going to teach her," said Lydia. "She's exceptional, you know. You've noticed her over here, haven't you?"

"I've noticed there are two of you," replied the renter. He had a martial jaw and his skin was the color of vanilla. He looked like at some time or another he might have been an army officer, maybe stationed in the Panama Canal Zone. That had to be the reason for his tallowed shade.

Across the street Rucelle was giving Annabelle and Elzora Dragoo a little lawn party. A tasseled beach umbrella had been set up and a card table and three chairs had been placed beneath it. The snowy cake on the table looked like it might be coconut. The lawn sprinklers had been turned on and while Rucelle fussed with cake plates and silverware and napkins, Annabelle and Elzora, both in bathing suits, darted in and out of the falling water drops, turning cartwheels and shrieking. In a rainbow made by the sun and whirling water

Annabelle took a running leap, flipped over, and landed perfectly. "Wheeeeee! Isn't this some fun?"

"I heard your music a while ago," said Lydia to Footsie.

"Did you," said the renter. It wasn't a question. He was through transferring ladybugs from the carton to the plants. Weaving back and forth with each breath of the wind they appeared as dancers competing for their teacher's approval.

"You'll be glad to know," said Lydia, "I liked it. The man who wrote it must've been going through some kind of ordeal. That's what I thought when I heard it. Was he?"

"Yes," answered the renter. He was preparing to go back into his house, lifting his camp stool, stooping to part a path through the plants and vines. His bald head shone like a tan mirror in the sun and it occurred to Lydia that he must be a very arty man. He did not have the look of a person who went out and worked every day for his living and, as a matter of fact, she had never observed him either going in the morning or returning in the evening but only in his back yard in the afternoons.

"I'd like to know what his ordeal was," Lydia called to Footsie's departing back and on his threshold he paused and turned to answer, "He was deaf."

Deaf and still able to write music like that. How was it she knew beforehand the music hadn't come from any normal person? Lydia pulled her knees to her chin and sat balanced on the fence like a large, wise frog, blinking at Footsie's door which had closed behind him. The deaf composer's affliction must have been slow crucifixion for him. Probably he had been rich and able to afford the finest doctors and for years had run around trying to find one to help him. Not one could. In the end he had sat, stunned, alone, making up his mind. Thinking, I am alive and I might have to stay that way a long time. I want to be alive. I can still see and smell and taste. I can still care. Now I've got to make up my mind whether to care or say phooey on it. I can't say phooey on it; I haven't yet said all I was put here to say. I say phooey on them, all those smart-nosed doctors. What do they know? They've never been deaf. I've been knocked flat on my royal with this trouble but I know something they don't know. A man who's been knocked flat on his royal and told he's got nowhere else to go has got it on his side. The difference between you and me, doctor, is I've had this ordeal handed to me. A man with an ordeal will make it, that's the difference. He's mad. You better not do any messing around with him. He's a barracuda. Doctor, to know what people like me are all about you got to get yourself a cross and cart it around a while. I notice you haven't got one. You better pray to sweet Jesus you never get one. I doubt you could go around the block with it. Only people like me and Lydia Birdsong can do that. We know what it's all about. We got us an ordeal. Got us a mountain. Gonna knock that mountain down. Yayhoooooooo.

Lydia jumped down from the fence and went inside and looked at her sister. How was it she could go to sleep so quick just any old where and stay that way so long? What did that smile mean? That she felt pleasure? Or pain? You never could tell. Maybe it meant she was plotting some devilment. Today might be the day she would again take the garden shears and finish murdering the gardenia bushes that grew on the south side of the house. Or maybe she would tiptoe to the utility house and sit in a puddle of green paint, leaning to smear her face and hair in it. You could never tell about Lornie. The house could be perfectly still and quiet and then, all of a sudden, if you hadn't been watching and listening, you might smell smoke or look in the bathroom and see it flooded and Lornie would be hiding under a bed with her hands pressed to her grinning mouth. Appeals were useless. Lornie didn't understand danger or the cost of things. Didn't understand much about love, only the dependency side of that.

In her sleep Lornie put her legs straight up in the air and said, "Clush."

"Shhhhhh," said Lydia. "You're home now. For all summer. Isn't that nice? We're going to have some good times, I promise you. But we're going to do some hard work too, I promise you that also."

"Mumph," said Lornie and let her legs fall and sat up and opened her eyes. "Oh," she said in a dark, piquant tone, "it's you." Her hair hadn't been done properly. It hung straight down from her scalp to the tips of her earlobes and in the front was parted, creating a little draped stage for her face. She still had her square, brown school shoes on. The laces were untied and so was the belt to her dress which the teachers at the school insisted be old-maid length, long enough to cover her knees. Beneath the dress there was a cotton slip and a pair of snuggies—plain white pants that came down to the middle of her thighs.

"Hiya," said Lydia. "You awake now?"

Lornie cast her a sideways, isolated look, drew her feet up to rest flat on the throw rug and began the troubled effort of tying her shoelaces.

"When somebody says hiya to you you're supposed to say hiya back," said Lydia.

"Hiya," said Lornie.

"It's too hot for those big old square shoes," said Lydia. "Why don't you take them off and go barefooted? That's what I do. See? I take my shoes off in June and I don't put them back on till September. I don't wear clothes either, not any more'n I can help. Whoever invented them oughta be guillotined."

Still holding the same steady, worried expression, Lornie gathered the loose ends of her shoelaces. She threaded them backwards through the metal shoe eyes.

"You don't need those heavy shoes, Lornie. They're too hot for summer. Take them off."

"No," protested Lornie. "I do this. By myself. Daddy say so."

In a voice louder and more emphatic than she had intended it to be, Lydia said, "Daddy's gone away for a while, Lornie." As if she had been hit from behind she coughed.

Lornie's fingers, wrestling with the shoelaces, stilled for a second, then were involved in the task again.

"Didn't Muzz tell you?"

"Yer, yer, yer," answered Lornie. She was finished with one shoe. She thrust her foot out for Lydia to see the lopsided bow.

Lydia said, "That's fine, but you don't have to do the other one. Daddy won't get mad at you. He's gone away for a while. I'm going to be your boss now. Take off those shoes. Don't you want to? Aren't they hot?"

"Yer," said Lornie and pulled both shoes off and dropped them.

"You got to get comfortable like I am," said Lydia, jumping over to the clothes chest to pull a pair of underpants, shorts, and a shirt from one of the drawers. "No wonder they couldn't teach you anything at that school. They were too busy worrying about if somebody was going to see you with some of your parts exposed. Ha! What's so secret how we look underneath our clothes? We're all cut out of the same stuff. You got to be comfortable while you're livin' and learnin', that's my motto. Tsch. Snuggies in this kind of weather. Fantastic. Take them off. See me? You want to be like me, don't you? Free and graceful?"

"Yer, yer, yer," said Lornie, thrusting her face, inspired. The brief, white underpants, wash-worn shorts, and boxy shirt transformed her from an institution schoolgirl to a kid on summer vacation. Lydia brushed her hair back and up and made her a hair sprout like her own, held in place with a wide rubber band.

Presently Lydia and her sister sat on the front porch steps, Lydia watching the street for Billy Frank and Lornie looking across to where Rucelle Blue and the Dragoo kids sat under their umbrella eating cake and drinking cold drinks. Lornie's eyes followed their every movement.

"Don't watch them," said Lydia. "Don't give them that satisfaction. Look at the trees. Aren't they pretty and green?"

"Hmppppmph," said Lornie with her eyes still trained on the scene across the street.

"I am sitting here and I am reconnoitering," said Lydia. "Tomorrow morning, right after we eat our breakfast, I am going to start teaching you. You don't need to worry, it won't be like it was with Daddy. I won't get mad at you when you don't understand and we won't hurry and I'll be right there every minute. We'll study together till noon, then we'll eat lunch, then we'll go somewheres. Downtown or to Froggy Pond. How does that sound to you?"

"Yer," said Lornie. "They havin' fun 'n' games." And before Lydia could stop her she jumped from the steps, ran down the walk, and was through the gate and across the street, darting up onto the Dragoos' lawn where Rucelle, Annabelle, and Elzora sat eating their cake and drinking their cold drinks.

Lydia stood up and yelled, "Lornie, come back.

Come on back over here. I don't want you over there."

Rucelle and the two Dragoo kids had got to their feet and the impression was that Rucelle thrust her two charges behind her, protecting them, though there was actually no move in that direction. From her position Lydia could not make out Rucelle's expression but she knew what kind it would be—a revolting mixture of curiosity and coy sympathy.

"Lornie," hollered Lydia, going down the steps. "You come on back over here where you belong. I don't want you over there, you hear?" She might just as well have saved her breath for all the attention Lornie paid.

Accompanied by Coochie Pepper, Billy Frank was coming around the corner of the far end of the street. He was pulling a child's wagon which contained a glass tank and two big glass jars, and Coochie, in a white dress and long, pink scarf, walked alongside. Coochie had eyes the color of fresh green peas and claimed to be able to receive messages from the spirits of the dead. She attended funerals as some people attended movies and knew every person in every cemetery in the town by his first name.

Seeing Lornie was not about to obey her order, Lydia went across the street after her. Rucelle stood with her right arm around Annabelle and her left one around Elzora and when Lydia was within speaking distance she said, "She didn't mean any harm now, Lydia. Don't scold her. Not on our account."

"I wasn't going to," said Lydia and reached for

Lornie's hand. "Come on now, let's go home. Look. Lookit there who's coming. There's Billy Frank and Coochie."

Lornie grinned and allowed herself to be led back across the street and she and Lydia stood in front of the Birdsongs' gate waiting for Billy Frank and Coochie. They came on slowly, Billy Frank being careful with his cargo. When he and Coochie were abreast of the Birdsongs' gate he pulled up and stopped. He hadn't so much as glanced in the direction of the Dragoos' yard and neither had Coochie. Coochie said to Lornie, "Hey, honey. How you doing?"

"Flllllpt," said Lornie.

"I've been to the most gorgeous funeral," Coochie said. "There were so many flowers there wasn't enough room for all the people."

"Billy Frank," said Lydia, "Rucelle's in the Dragoos' yard watching you."

"I hope she gets her eyes full," said Billy Frank. "Open the gate for me."

"She's fixing to come over here," warned Lydia.

"Let her," said Billy Frank. "I'll kill her, she does any messing around with me. Open the gate, Lyddy. Coochie, you coming in or you going on?"

"I can't make up my mind," said Coochie. "I know I ought to go home but I don't want to. Tom Ben's out selling real estate and it's lonely with just me there."

"You shouldn't go to so many funerals," remarked Billy Frank. Lydia had opened the gate but he was making no move to take the wagon through. He had knelt beside it and was looking at the two glass jars, each containing one ribbon seahorse floating in pale green seawater, some fine bottom sand, and some blades of sea grass. Squinting, he pressed both hands to his cheeks. One of the seahorses clinging to a blade of sea grass had begun to bend sharply backward and forward.

The light from the sky was of the truest value of the day, colored pure saffron, and the renter across the way, Footsie, was again playing the ordeal music of the deaf composer. Scarred, an argument with the unseen, a violent argument that was in some electric fashion related to those clustered now around the little wobbly wagon. They observed that one of the little seahorses was giving birth. With each exertion of his body there came from his brood pouch under his tail a baby seahorse, perfectly formed.

"My Lord," said Coochie. She was squatting between Lornie and Billy Frank.

To her twin Lydia said, "Look, Lornie. Look at the little seahorse. Isn't he the cutest little fella? He's having babies."

"Yer, yer, yer," said Lornie, preserving her look of isolation.

Rucelle was coming across the street. Lydia and Coochie looked up at the same time and saw this. If she had half the sense of a nanny goat she'd leave this alone, thought Lydia. And Coochie said, "I knew I should've gone on. Why didn't I? Lord, I hate and despise trouble."

Rucelle's feet brought her across the street and they lifted her up on the curb and carried her to within a foot of Billy Frank. He did not raise his head. Rucelle said, "Billy Frank."

"Go 'way," said Billy Frank. "Nobody asked you over here." While appearing to be still fully absorbed with the seahorse he had his eyebrows pulled down and was studying his thumbs.

Rucelle said, "Billy Frank, you get this wagon turned around and get on back home with it."

"Why?" said Billy Frank. The look on his face was positive and dangerous. He still hadn't looked at Rucelle. "Why?" he asked. "It's my wagon and what's in it is mine and these are my friends."

"I don't want to embarrass you in front of your friends," said Rucelle. "It's a private matter why you should take your wagon and go home. I'll talk to you about it in private. This evening."

"I am twelve years old," said Billy Frank, "and I am not breaking any laws or hurting anybody. I might not be home till ten o'clock so you got anything to say to me you better say it now. What's it about?"

Rucelle shook her head. "I can't tell you. Not here. Not now. It's private, I told you."

"Nobody," said Billy Frank boldly and with conviction, "knows what kind of kids they're going to have till they get here. If you wasn't so ignorant you'd know that, Rucelle." He had leaned forward and was looking at Rucelle intently. "If you wasn't so ignorant you'd know you wasn't perfect. Nobody is. It wasn't your idea to be born normal. It wasn't anybody's. It just happened. It could happen the other way around just as easy. Why don't you think about it once in a while? Why don't you think what'll happen if you and Harley Bell have a kid that isn't normal? What'll you do with him? Hide him from the neighbors? Drown him?"

"Oh, you nasty boy," said Rucelle, and Billy Frank sprang up and over the wagon and was on Rucelle so quickly she staggered backward. She couldn't shake him off. She stepped first one way and then another and he followed her, clinging with one hand and pounding with the other. He did this as if he had rehearsed it all in his mind and he had his lips drawn back from his teeth in an evil grimace and it was an ugly thing to watch.

"My Lord," murmured Coochie. "Should we try and stop him?"

"Billy Frank!" said Lydia. "Billy Frank!"

Billy Frank had Rucelle down on the sidewalk and they were rolling. Billy Frank was hitting Rucelle methodically and he wasn't being particular about where. One of her pearl earbobs popped off, flew up into the air, and landed at Lydia's feet. Rucelle was screaming and trying to fight back but not making much headway; Billy Frank was too strong for her. Finally he had her flat on the sidewalk and sprawled on her stomach holding her arms down with his hands and her legs down with his feet. All of this had only taken a minute or so but Rucelle was thoroughly whipped.

The Dragoo kids were standing on their curb silently observing. They looked like they might want to come to Rucelle's aid but she called out to them ordering them to stay where they were. She was crying. "Oh, you wait. You just wait, Billy Frank Blue. You're going to be sorry. I'm your sister. When you had the measles that time you think you wouldn't have died if I hadn't stayed home from school and nursed you?"

"I didn't ask you to," said Billy Frank. "I was too little to talk when I had the measles."

"I was only a baby myself," squalled Rucelle. "And you were so cute and I loved you but look at you now. Just look at you! You just wait till Daddy hears about this."

Billy Frank said, "He'll hear about it 'cause I'll tell him myself. Don't mess with me, Rucelle, and leave my friends alone. If I want to marry one of them when I get old enough I will." He then let Rucelle up and returned to his former position beside the wagon acting as if nothing at all had happened. Rucelle tottered back across the street to the Dragoos' yard and sat in a chair beneath the tasseled umbrella and let Annabelle and Elzora comfort her.

To Lydia and the others knotted in front of the Birdsongs' gate Billy Frank said, "All right, it wasn't anything. You all needn't look at me like that. Come on, help me get this stuff inside. This aquarium should've been hooked up to the electricity thirty minutes ago. That water's got to be aerated else my animals will die."

Nobody moved. Lornie had an end of Coochie's pink scarf in her hands and was holding it to her nose sniffing its perfume. Coochie was looking at Billy Frank as if he had suddenly become some kind of a marvel. She said, "You know, life is full of heroism. Listen, Sugar, have you got any dead ancestors you might want to talk to sometime?"

"I don't think so," replied Billy Frank. "If my dead ones are like my live ones I'd just as soon forget it."

Feeling such a giddy rush of praise and emotion for Billy Frank as to be almost swamped with it, Lydia did an idiotic thing. With her neck thrust to a grotesque angle and her arms flopping because all of a sudden she didn't know what to do with them she lunged at Billy Frank crying, "Take me with you to the Arctic when you go! Don't leave me here by myself!"

five

Till then Lornie's conduct, her habits and beliefs and impulses, had not been any great concern of Lydia's. Those had belonged to her parents and it hadn't been up to her to interfere, to say what struck her as being right and what struck her as being wrong. Her life, of course, had been a part of the lives of the members of her family and yet she had always lived it a little apart from them, keeping her secrets secret and not confiding in anyone, not even Billy Frank, her innermost impressions of the world. Not because they were so weighty or anything like that but because they were fickle and this was embarrassing. One day her imagination would be possessed by a thing or an idea and, irresistibly, she would spend hours thinking about it and drawing plans around it only to waken in the beginning of the next day and be disgusted with it. Ten hundred times this had happened.

It seemed to her the profitable thing to do would be to feel the same way all the time so as to give her feelings and thoughts about things a chance to become absolute, but so far realization of this ambition had eluded her. Her impressions of life and people were coquettish and this was disquieting and she couldn't change their rulings.

There was another troubling thing and this concerned purpose. Sometimes while moseying around the back passages of the town she would look up and meet the eyes of another and feel an overwhelming sympathy for him and all people, for it seemed to her, especially in this year it seemed to her, nobody knew their purpose and everybody was wasting his days, the same as she, waiting for revelation. For the sun to flare suddenly and then a sorcered voice from it to speak. For the glacial ice of the Arctic to come sliding down, melting, creeping over the land, causing gorges bigger and grander than the Grand Canyon and creating another sea. Causing the earth to warp and be thrust upward to the sky. Then, while everybody was up there all thrown together, maybe the meaning of the world would be revealed. The reasons for its oceans, its rocks and monsoons, and why some people are born quirks.

In a bygone time when she had had other friends besides Billy Frank they had asked, "What is wrong with your sister?" And she had replied, "She is exceptional. She is a trick of nature." It had not been enough to say that. They wanted to know why and how and what. She could not say why and how and what and so she and the friends, who had not been friends at all, parted company.

Now it was a different time and the days in it were changed. It was nine o'clock in the morning of this day and the teaching of Lornie was about to begin. Lydia and her sister sat at the table which stood near the window in their bedroom. The hard, brilliant sun illuminated the window and was like a white spotlight on the other side of its green, half-drawn blind. From the window the scenery was mainly of yard, fence, and sky. On the other side of the fence Footsie's house was quiet; the whole neighborhood was quiet.

Lydia and her sister sat on opposite sides of the table looking at each other. There was no expectancy in Lornie's eyes. They merely accepted what she saw. Right after breakfast she had spent a considerable time in the bathroom applying a thick white face cream to her cheeks and eyelids and she had wet the ends of her hair sprout and put bath powder on her neck. Now she sat with her hands folded before her and every once in a while a drop of the melting cream would roll down from one of her eyelids like a clown's tear.

The meaning of the situation was enormous. Lydia felt that and yet its true worth was being denied her.

She was afraid of how much Lornie didn't know and of her own ignorance and there was no one to ask was this the right way to begin or if she should begin at all. Why was it she always had to think she could do the things others could not?

Her harmonica was lying on the table and she picked it up intending, for inspiration, to try and draw one of the long, sweet notes of Footsie's deaf composer. Instead it came out like a bang on a tin can. She laid the instrument aside. "Well, well," she said. "Here we are at school and it's the first day. We have to pretend that. Isn't that nice? Speaking for myself I think it's amazing. I never thought I'd want to be a teacher but now, all of a sudden, that's all I want to be. Isn't that funny? When I say funny I mean peculiar. Do you know the difference between those two words, Lornie?"

"Yer," replied Lornie and for her own reason shivered.

"What's the difference?"

"Funny is when the laugh," said Lornie, wagging her head from side to side, and cut loose with the longest string of words, the longest story Lydia had ever heard come from her. "Ha ha. I know. Miss King at school she always laugh. Ho ho. Heh heh. Ha ha. She knows I ascared when I go to sleep. YUH yuh yuh yuh. I pinched her and she say HO, ho, ho, ho. When we go over the street and Janie got with us and everybody and the car came and the woman had a cat and he got out. Whufffffft. He ran up Miss King's dress. And she said ERRRRRRK. And the mans stopped the car.

CRUUUUUUK. Miss King she was mad. The cat he ran up her laig and she snktttttt. She hit him. He fell off. The cat he . . . I hit Miss King. She said everybody get off and everybody get off and we go over the street back and Miss King say to me why did you hit me and I say the cat. He was hurted. And she say ho, ho, ha, ha, heh, heh and I say put a dirty dishrag on your nose ha, ha, and Miss King knows I like lemonade and she say no lemonade for you and she didn't give me any and she knows I don't like dark by myself and she said to Janie you don't sleep here any more with Lornie."

For a long moment Lydia regarded her twin. Except for the eyes it was like looking at her own image in a mirror. Nothing could be judged by looking into Lornie's eyes. They spoke no language, carried on with nothing.

If I could be her, thought Lydia. She tried to imagine herself in the switched role. I am sitting here now and I am Lornie. There is something in my brain that keeps me from knowing things. Like a door that's been nailed shut. I don't care what's on the other side of the door. Why? Because I only know what's on this side so I think this is all and it isn't very interesting. There was Miss King. And Janie. There is Muzz. There was Daddy. There's my sister. Up to now I lived in my school but two days every week I got to come home. When I got here they said eat and I ate. They said sleep and I slept. Muzz said you're Mama's baby. Who wants to be a baby all his life? My sister does not know me much. I am in her way; she has to take me places and explain me. Daddy said learn. That's all he wanted from me. I could. If people didn't holler at me. If they loved me first.

Lydia laid fingers on her throbbing temples. Her brain whirled round and she was herself again but something had taken place. This was a beginning of some kind. Something was expected of her.

It was so quiet in the room, so quiet Lydia could hear the blood running through her veins. She leaned toward Lornie and as if to hypnotize her, fixed her with an unblinking stare. "Listen, Lornie, how things were before is finished now. There's just you and me now and things are different. You know why? It's because we're buddies now. Real good buddies."

A drop of the face cream slid down from Lornie's cheek to her chin line. It dropped on the collar of her shirt. "The cat," she murmured.

"We're going to get you a cat," promised Lydia. "A nice sweet old pawchie. Coochie will know where we can get one for nothing. But did you hear what I said just now? Did you hear me when I said we're buddies now?"

"Yer."

"That means I'll do anything for you. Anything. I want you to be like me. You want to, don't you?"

"Yer."

"We'll show them," said Lydia and stood up but then sat down again quickly. She felt drunk with ambition. The learning cards once used by her father to try to teach Lornie were on the table before her and she reached and pawed through them, selecting one. "Okay, now we got all that out of the way we can start. You remember these word cards? You remember these, Lornie? Lookit, Lornie. Look at this card and tell me what you see."

"Box," said Lornie.

"No."

"Yer."

"This is not a picture of a box, Lornie. It's a picture of a house."

Lornie shrugged.

"Okay, we got that one settled let's go on to the next one. Look, Lornie, what is this?"

"Banana."

"No. You didn't look. How can you say what you think it is till you've looked? Look at it, Lornie."

"Banana."

"No."

"Bicycle."

"No."

"What?"

"Lornie, it's your job to tell me, not mine to tell you. You're supposed to look at the card and tell me what you see."

Lornie let her head lie on her shoulder. She stared at the card upheld. "Book."

"No."

"Yer."

"Why do you keep saying that? When somebody shows you a picture of a boat and it is a boat you're not supposed to argue with them. This isn't a case of the halt leading the blind. I know a boat when I see one. And stop saying yer when you mean yes. That's not a word."

"I wanna drink."

"In a minute. How can you be thirsty? You only had breakfast half an hour ago. Listen, Lornie, let me explain something to you. This is school like a real school. The only difference is that it's here and not in a school building. Now we got to act like we're in a real school. I'm the teacher and you're the pupil. Now we've just decided this boat is a boat. So now we take this next card and you tell me what—"

"I wanna drink."

"I told you, in a minute. First—"

"I wanna drink."

"Sweet Jesus, there's no justice. All right, go get one. No, I'll go get it for you. You wait here. Don't move. I'll be right back."

The whole morning was an exercise in frustration. After three trips to the kitchen for glasses of iced water Lydia lugged in a full pail and set it and a cup beside the table. "Now then, when you want a little drink it'll be right there. Drink all you want. Water's good for you. I hope there's nothing wrong with your kidneys. Did we finish with the cards?"

"Yer," said Lornie, fishing an ice cube from the bucket. She pushed it into her mouth and sucked. She rolled the cube around in her mouth and rolled her eyes. She crunched the ice with her teeth and chewed it. One by one she fished all the ice cubes from the bucket of water and ate them and took no more notice of Lydia than if she had been a fly on the wall.

Lydia stacked the learning cards and while waiting for Lornie to be through with her messing tried to imagine herself as a deaf person. It was impossible because the neighborhood had come awake. Annabelle and Elzora Dragoo had come out of their house and were roller skating in the street; they were experts at this, skimming and whizzing, making fancy little turns. Their brief skirts showed off their cute legs and their hair, the color of maple syrup, shone in the sun. Ten and twelve years old, they were thicker than thieves. Never apart, always with their arms around each other. Lydia removed her eyes from the scene. Today her feelings about the Dragoos were bloodless.

Lydia sat with her feet hooked around the legs of her chair and her chin in her hand gazing at Lornie who was finished with the ice. The front of her shirt was wet and her lips were pink-chilled. She had drawn back into her chair and her hands were quiet in her lap and her eyes drowsed.

The sun had moved away from the window and school was out for that day for the pupil had gone away. It had been a waste. The waste of Lornie sat in the room with Lydia, a raw and delicate presence. With the tip of her pencil Lydia spread the learning cards and one slid from the table and landed in the bucket of water and in that same instant the music of Footsie's deaf composer started. He was home and playing the record again. The strains of it came out of his windows and across the fence and into the Birdsongs' house and the knowledge beating in it was like the beating of an older, extra heart. The heart must touch the heart, that is where the power lives.

Lydia said, "Lornie, honey."

"Lemme," said Lornie, half-asleep, her chin drooping on her shoulder.

"Lornie, talk to me. I have to talk to you about something very important."

"Lemme," said Lornie. Her breathing was peaceful, she didn't open her eyes.

"Lornie," said Lydia. "I have to tell you something. It'll help you if you listen, it'll help us both. It's about how I feel about you. I love you."

The expression on Lornie's face remained the same. Unlittered. Her mystery and the meaning of her a big and terrible challenge to the mind and imagination. Footsie's music was in the room and it was inside Lydia's head, ancient and then young, a long, great tide pouring, encircling the world. Lydia put her arms on the table and lowered her head to them and presently the thickening heat of the day and Lornie's sleep-whistlings and gruntings put her to the brink of a queer twilight.

It was not a gentle, restoring time, this hour. Her perceptions did not dim and rest as they do in true sleep but came gliding from their graveyards and there was no choice but to look at them for there was no way to see around them or through them, they were so thick. They called to her, "Lydiaaaaaaaaaa."

"What?" she whispered, swimming, struggling between consciousness and unconsciousness. "What is it?"

They carried lighted lanterns and they rose up out of a gray, bubbling swamp. They came toward her swinging their lights. They formed a circle around her and fell to their knees. One spoke. "Lydia, why do you lie?"

"I don't," she whispered. "Never. I do love her. I do. I do."

They laughed, unbelieving, and the swamp hissed and swallowed them and the sound of her own watery voice, unbelieving also, roused her to wakefulness. "I do love her. I do. I do." Spoken with that special emphasis one gives to BIG LIES.

In the aftermath of the dream Lydia was exceedingly generous, allowing Lornie at lunch to eat all of the tuna fish salad and all but a tablespoon of the peach ice cream.

six

In those first days of this time of significance Lydia's ambitions for Lornie burned in her like a new fire, yet she did not speak of them to Muzz for in proper secrecy there lies strength. When you blab your intentions they weaken and take on a look and feeling of confusion. Also there was the question of failure. What if, in the end, there was failure? Then she would have to say, "Daddy was right. She cannot learn. She is hopeless. I don't blame him for running away. What else could he do?"

Whenever Lydia allowed herself the luxury of

thinking of her father it was at night. She would not let him pass through her mind in the daytime for broodings of him deserved full attention. At night this occupation wasn't interrupted. She would lie in her bed waiting for Lornie's sleep-sputterings to begin and then, after their pattern was established, she would fold her hands on her stomach, close her eyes, and wait, as you wait in a movie house, for the first flashing announcement. Her father, hung in rags and looking ravenous and haunted, would appear on the screen. A voice would say, "It's him! Fire the pot!" And another would say, "No, keep the crowds back. Every man has the right to be heard. Can't you see this poor devil is suffering?"

"Not enough!" screamed the people. They wanted to boil him in oil and would have but a girl came from the shadows and said, "Stop. I command you to set this man free. His punishment has been decreed. He will wander the face of the earth till time stops and even the dull and ignorant will look on him in loathing. No person will ever touch him again or even the animals in the forest. His soul will never know peace again. He will have no home. Children will shrink from him."

There was a whole series of these plays and she rehearsed them every night until sleep overcame her. Soon she had favorites. Her roles in these pageants got shifted around quite a bit. In one she was a psychiatrist renowned for her work with exceptional children and six doctors from Norway and two from Germany came. The doctors said, "You must tell us your secret. We will pay you any amount of money." She curled her lip and replied, "Fools. Do not insult me with your offers of money. I will tell you my secret for nothing. It is LOVE and it is putting yourself in the place of these kids. You have got to let these exceptional ones know you love them and you have to learn how to speak their language. That is how I teach."

In another of her mind-plays her father returned alone but she could never get beyond the point where he stood in the doorway with his mouth hanging open, unable to tell the difference between her and Lornie. Something blocked the development of that one.

Her father did not write and he did not send for the rest of his clothes. To Muzz Lydia said, "Wouldn't you think he'd at least come back for the rest of his clothes?"

"I'm not surprised he hasn't," said Muzz, shredding salad greens into a bowl. "Where's Lornie?"

"Watching television. Where do you think he is?"

"Maybe California," said Muzz. "Or New Mexico. He has some cousins out there. I never met them but your father used to talk about them."

"A lot of people get amnesia," said Lydia. "You can just be walking by a building and somebody can drop something on your head, a brick or something like that, and then you can't remember who you are or anything about yourself."

"Lyddy," said Muzz, "wherever your father is you can be sure he's in charge of all his faculties. He isn't sick. He's in good health. He is where he is because that's where he wants to be."

"I don't see how you can know that," said Lydia, not really expecting to be furnished any more light on the subject. So it shocked her when Muzz, taking a pan of baked apples from the oven, said, "All right, you might as well know. I know it because this isn't the first time your father has walked out on us. It's happened twice before. The first time when you and Lornie were two and the second time when you were three." The words fell like the strokes of a little hammer in the warm, quiet room. They did not accuse or ask for sympathy but merely told what had to be the truth; they had that ring to them.

Lydia reacted as she did when she was reading and had an unpleasant truth revealed to her. She tasted it and backed away from it but still it was there, part of the knowledge of the world and not to be ignored. She had been setting the table for the evening meal and lifted her eyes and met those of her mother. "Why," she said, "I think that's so funny. I always thought I knew him because he was my father but I didn't. I only know the things he taught me."

"I am sorry," said Muzz. "I am just so very sorry. I'm not trying to turn you against your father but only trying to help you see things as they are."

Lornie ate two of the baked apples topped with blobs of whipped cream for her supper, chopping them with her spoon until they were mush and then holding the dish to her mouth, letting the fruit and cream slide in. Some of the mixture slipped down on her chin and, watching her, Muzz did not correct her, but kept touching her napkin to her own mouth. She talked about her day at the hospital, laughing and inviting Lydia and Lornie to laugh with her, at some of the funny things she told, and the supper was like a hundred, a thousand others had been. Except when it was completed there was one thing different. There was the answer to an old loafer-puzzler in Lydia's mind, one that had escaped positive identification for years.

There were the empty dishes and the oncoming dusk making shades in the windows and the answer to the puzzler was this: Muzz did not love Lornie, not truly. To Muzz, Lornie was a punishment the same as she had been a punishment to Dad. How could Lydia know this? Listen. The eye does not always deliver its messages to the brain. Sometimes, especially sometimes when you are a child, it is possible to look at a thing or a person and look again and yet again and perceive only the outside of the thing or the person. But then some day or some night you hear a word or a phrase or catch a truant look and you are jolted from ignorance to realization. It's like discovering the reasoning in mathematics. The mystery is finally solved. It all makes sense.

When Lydia made her discovery about Muzz she felt her childhood leave her; it fell away from her like an extra skin. It must have showed because Muzz said, "What is it? Headache?" And Lydia replied yes and was required to swallow a pill. After the dishes were done she sat alone on the front steps feeling fragile, feeling herself insufficient, feeling forsaken and somehow blemished in a way beyond her recognition.

Just before full darkness Billy Frank's mother and father came for his aquarium. To Muzz Mr. Blue said, "There's nothing personal in this, you understand. We haven't got a thing against Billy Frank being friends with Lydia; she hasn't done anything. It's Billy Frank. He's got to be a real handful, so starting tomorrow he's going to Bible school and when he gets done with that we'll figure out something else to keep him off the streets."

While they were loading the glass tank and related paraphernalia into their car Lydia sat on the steps watching them and concealing the contempt she felt for them. She smiled at them and offered a silent prayer of thanksgiving to God. Thank you, God. Thank you, thank you, thank you for not making me like those two old warthogs. Or like Rucelle or the Dragoos. I would rather be exceptional and not know the difference between a bicycle and a banana. Help me, God, to show Lornie the difference.

In the beginning of this time Lydia found herself on more personal terms with God than she had ever been before. Secretly she harbored a skulking suspicion that her past sins stood somewhat in the way between her and any heavenly bounty but this carried its own reward. It strengthened her ambitions. There was a streak of toughness in her that pushed her along on the crest of an unfathomable conviction, deep and primitive. About Lornie she could not say to herself, Cure is impossible. She thought, It is possible. Lornie is a part of me so I know this. One time, before we separated, we were as one, sharing the same heart and blood, and this is how I know this thing I know.

Each morning, soon after dawn, Muzz left for work and then Lydia was up and pulling at Lornie to rise also. Lornie never wanted to rise. She had to be dragged from her bed. If there were boiled eggs for breakfast she wanted poached and if there was cereal she wanted pancakes. Anything to delay the time when Lydia would put her harmonica to her lips and blow two loud, businesslike blasts which meant school, ready or not. Lornie was never ready. She would scream from the bathroom, "Yer, yer!" Or from the kitchen, "You are deaf me! Quit!" And then after some silence come limping from one of those rooms to the classroom and sit across the table from Lydia yawning, uncaring about the answer to her question but asking it anyway. "Why wer to do this?"

"I'll tell you again," said Lydia. "Because you're twelve now, same as me, but you don't know half the things I know. Now let's reconnoiter. In plain English that means size up the situation. Before long you'll be saying words like that, that's what I got in mind for you. Now the size of the situation this morning is, you talk like a foreigner."

"Dasht?" said Lornie, her oiled face agleam. She

75

had soaped her hair sprout so that it stood in the center of her scalp like a white candle and had scrubbed her ears until they were red.

"A foreigner," continued Lydia, "is somebody from South America or China or someplace like that and when he gets to this country he just keeps on talking his own language and has a terrible time because nobody can understand what he means. He can't even go to the store to buy anything because he can't read our language. Some foreigners are smart but they can't let anybody know it because they don't know how to talk our language. That's the way I got it figured out and I bet I'm right."

"Yerrrrrr," assented Lornie.

"Your hair looks nice," said Lydia. "So do your ears. Well, let's see. We were talking about language. Listen, Lornie, yer is not a word. You've got to stop saying it. When you mean yes you should say yes, not yer."

Lornie put her locked hands on her forehead. She set her severe gaze on Lydia's face. The rays of the sun lighted the window.

"Now then," said Lydia. "We're going to use the cards again. I've made up a little story around them and I'm going to tell it to you and when I get done you can tell it back to me and then I'll be able to think what I have to do next. Don't interrupt me while I'm talking. Don't stop me and say you want a drink of water. Here's a whole bucketful with ice in it and here's a cup. When you want a drink you just kick the bucket like this and I'll reach down and get you one. Don't you do it, you spill too much. Now then, you ready?"

Lornie did not nod or shake her head. She swallowed cautiously.

Lydia held the learning cards and began to exhibit them as she talked, giving emphasis to the special words. "This is a *house* and a family like us lives in it. There is a *mother* and a *daddy* and two *children*. They have *trees* in their yard. There are some *birds* and every day when it gets too hot the *birds* go to sleep in the *trees*. *Birds* live in *trees*; people live in *houses*."

As if in some kind of agony, Lornie pressed her hands to her forehead and chewed her lips. She slid forward in her chair, narrowing her eyes. "Whut—?"

"I told you not to interrupt me, Lornie, and you have. Do you hurt somewhere? Are you sick?"

"Ner," said Lornie and shuddered for her own reason.

"Listen," said Lydia. "I'm going to talk some plain English to you. It's time somebody did. I'm not going to yell at you like Daddy did but I'm not going to treat you like Muzz does either, like you're still a baby. You aren't; you're almost grown. You're as old as I am. I want you to be like me. Don't you want to be like me?"

"Yer," whispered Lornie. "Yes. Me too."

"You had a question," said Lydia, "and when I get through with my story you can ask it. That's the way you have to do in regular school. Now. This family has a lot of *books*. They do not have a *boat*. They live in a *house*. The *father* goes to work every day and the *mother* goes to work every day and the *children* go to school every day except when it's summer. There is a little park near their *house* and sometimes the *mother* and *father* take the *children* there to look at the *squirrels* and *fish* and *birds* and *flowers*. This family is very happy. The *children* have a *bicycle*. They like to eat *bananas* and they write with *pencils*." Lydia placed the cards on the table. "That's the end and you can now ask your question. What was the question you wanted to ask me?"

"I wuz," said Lornie, trying to squirm out of the obligation. "You did ner say—"

"You wuz what? I didn't say what?"

Lornie let her hands slide from her forehead down over her nose to her mouth. She drew her lips in and pulled her breath in and considered. Finally she spoke. "You didn't say ther name."

Their name. What was the happy family's name? Why was she supposed to know it, nobody else did. Why did they have to have one? Because everything in this world goes by a label and if you can't call it, if you happen to be a little quirky and can't rattle it off the minute somebody asks, you might just as well go live with the monkeys.

"Their name," said Lydia, inspired with genius, "was Bird."

"Humph," said Lornie.

"So help me," said Lydia. "And now we got that amazing fact out of the way you can tell me the story back. Here are the cards. Use the cards like I did. No, not the banana first. Start with the house. Oh well, start with the banana."

"The banana," said Lornie, speaking softly, bending her head to gaze at the card. "Miss King she ride the bicycle. Ha ha. Heh heh. HO HO HO. She lppppppppd! Craaaaaaaak! Janie she looked and did her eye down like this and I looked and did my eye down like this and OH!" Lornie squinted her eyes and then they flamed and then, all of a sudden, she threw herself backward in her chair. It went over and she rolled on the floor, her sides heaving.

"Get up," said Lydia three times and each time her order only worsened the situation. It was kind of awful to see that kind of amusement, so silent and so far removed from everything funny. Large, weak tears stood in Lornie's eyes and she had half a fist in her mouth and the sight was disgusting.

Lydia could picture Miss King on the sidewalk with her head cracked open and the two little quirks squatted beside her, winking, enjoying themselves. Angered, she said, "Was Miss King hurt? Bad, I mean?"

Lornie got up and sat again in her chair. She thrust her neck out and her head hung from it at a contorted angle. She sprawled her legs and put her hands together in a praying gesture.

Dead, thought Lydia. Or maybe worse yet, paralyzed for life. How was it this little kink could not realize tragedy and show some feeling for it? She never showed any feeling for anybody. How was that? She

79

took feeling from others, their caring and love, but never gave any back. There was a reason, a reason, and if it could be found it might point the way to cure.

The sun coming through the green window blind was tingeing the white walls of the room green. It shone on her harmonica and she picked it up and held it. She had a tin ear and had never been able to play it expertly. The truth of the matter was she didn't have any real accomplishments. Even her lies, blabbered occasionally to strangers, lacked the polish and style good lies should have: *My sister has a rare disease which nobody else in my family has ever had or ever will have because it can only be inherited one time to a family and she's in a hospital in Quebec, Canada.*

The ordeal music of Footsie's deaf composer was in her head but piecemeal; she couldn't put the opening notes of it together. She raised the harmonica to her mouth and tried. aWAAAAAAAAH. aWAAAAAAAAH. Like a baby squalling.

But the other music. . . . There. There it was. Low and intense. Suffering. Through the darkness a long shape stealing. Then light, like birds flying. A painting. The dawn. A peek at the mystery. A plan.

Feeling very close to the mystery of Lornie, Lydia put the harmonica down and began to talk to Lornie about a hard subject. "Lornie," she asked. "Do you love anybody?"

Lornie jerked upright and again centered her attention on the learning cards. She picked two and, holding them aloft, intoned, "The father. . . . The mother. . . ."

"Lornie, do you love anybody?"

"The boat—"

"Lornie, don't you love Muzz? Daddy? Do you know what love is?"

"The house. . . . The family. . . . They eat the bananas."

"Oh, shut that up!" screamed Lydia. "Why can't you understand anything, you little quirk! I asked you if you knew what love is! I asked you if you loved anybody! Do you? Well, do you?"

"The children ride the bicycle," said Lornie in a suspicious, injured tone and kicked the water bucket so hard it went over and she didn't help mop up any of the spill.

After their cold, early lunch Lydia said, "Now, should we go to town or to Froggy Pond?" and when Lornie shrugged said, "Okay, we'll go to Froggy Pond."

They left their house and went across the street intending to cut through the Dragoos' side yard but Mrs. Dragoo called from one of her windows, "Lydia!"

Lydia reached for Lornie's hand. They were on the Dragoos' property, just barely, but still on it. The shape of Mrs. Dragoo loomed suddenly in a side window. "Lydia!"

Lydia shaded her eyes with her free hand.

"Ma'am? What d'you want? I can't see you very good. The sun's blinding me."

"Lydia," hollered Mrs. Dragoo, "I been meaning to talk to you about using my yard for a thoroughfare. I want you to quit it; you're ruining my grass."

"All right," screamed Lydia. "I won't do it anymore. It's hot, isn't it?"

"You wait right there," shouted Mrs. Dragoo. "There's a couple other things I been meaning to talk to you about. You wait right there."

"Kluck," said Lornie and with her bare feet pawed the clean grass and clasped her hands, grinding the palms of them together.

"Now we don't want any trouble with her," warned Lydia. "It *is* her grass and we're on it. Don't start anything, Lornie. Please don't try to start a fight. You can't win. Remember the time you and Elzora had that fight? Remember you lost? Somebody like you can't ever win a fight because you can't think fast enough. It's no disgrace though. Just think how nice it'd be if nobody could think fast enough to win a fight. Nobody'd ever start one because they'd know ahead of time nobody could win."

Lornie dropped her hands. She and Lydia stood and waited quietly and presently Mrs. Dragoo came fussing around the corner of her house, her eyes racing. She came out to where Lydia and Lornie waited. "I have to pay a man to keep this yard looking halfways decent and I don't want you using it for a racetrack any more," she said.

"I won't," said Lydia. "I told you I wouldn't any more."

Mrs. Dragoo inclined her head toward Lornie. "She understand what I'm talking about?"

Little, quick beads of excitement caused the muscles between Lydia's shoulder blades to jump. "Of course."

Mrs. Dragoo's manner turned. It was peculiar, unusually pleasant for her and with quite a bit of meaning in it. "I heard your father had left."

"Yes," said Lydia.

"Well," said Mrs. Dragoo, "we all have to do what we figure is best for ourselves."

"Yes," said Lydia.

"I don't suppose it was ever as easy for him as it looked. He was a good neighbor."

"He'll be back pretty soon," said Lydia. "His cousins in New Mexico needed him to come out there and advise them about their sheep ranch."

"God works in mysterious ways," said Mrs. Dragoo, glancing at Lornie.

"Yes," agreed Lydia. She thought, You old warthog. If Lornie wasn't standing here, if I didn't have to set the example for her, I'd fix your clock. I'd fix it so good it'd never run again. In her eyes Mrs. Dragoo appeared a blood-colored figure. She seemed to be doing a little floating dance, moving sideways and back and forth and turning. The sky seemed to be rolling. The trees at her back appeared to dip and sway, their arms lowering to embrace Mrs. Dragoo, to choke her.

83

Mrs. Dragoo was standing perfectly still. Nothing so worldly as a tree had better try any funny business with her. "Your father was a good neighbor," she repeated. "I am a good neighbor too. I never let my girls go where they aren't asked. I keep this place up and I don't listen to gossip and I teach my girls good manners. I pick what picture shows they can go to and what they can watch on television. There's too much wrong in the world these days and I don't want them to see any more of it than they have to. That's what I wanted to talk to you about. That and the grass."

"We won't use your yard for a shortcut any more," said Lydia, her senses stunned. To Lornie she said, "Come on, we can't go this way. We have to find another."

They had to go clear down to the end of the block and then make the turn onto a dirt road and the sand was so hot on their bare feet it actually seemed cold.

They went to Froggy Pond and like a couple of lost birds sat on one end of the railroad trestle. The farthest shore of the pond was fringed with hyacinths and spatterdock and above these blue and yellow flowers damselflies and dragonflies whirred in the orange sun.

"It's so hot I bet we could fry an egg on one of these rails," commented Lydia.

To this Lornie made no reply. Her soaped hair sprout had hardened and now appeared unrelated to the rest of her hair which hung in damp strings. Sweat on her forehead ran down the sides of her oiled cheeks.

If we sit here long enough, reflected Lydia, we

might have sunstrokes. I ought to take her home. What does she think sitting there like that so still? She must think something. What does she feel? She must be able to feel, the same as I. She hates that old warthog Dragoo, that's feeling. But good feelings? Doesn't she ever have good feelings about things and people? If I were her . . . Oh, I'm not her and I never can be. We are two separate people. Dear Jesus, am I going to fail with her the same as all the others?

Away on the distant skyscape a line of gray clouds was forming. It was going to rain. "It might rain," observed Lydia. "It won't hurt us any if it does, we aren't made of sugar." She took her harmonica from her pocket and blew a tune. aWAAAAAAAAH. aWAAAAAAAAH.

The clouds on the faraway horizon were banking, turning grayer, but still the sun continued to shine on the railroad trestle. Lornie sat with her head bent and her hands on her knees. She wasn't looking at what was beneath the trestle or watching the water in the pond or the bugs skimming around the heads of the water plants or anything. If I never spoke to her again that'd be all right with her, Lydia thought. She doesn't care. If God was to strike me dead right this minute she wouldn't care. She'd probably laugh.

In the distance lightning lighted the edges of the amassing clouds; they were far away and God was far away. The water in Froggy Pond was coming alive, little waves forming to run first toward the shore and then back again. Confused, they tumbled and swirled, and Lydia, looking down at them, did a crazy thing. There was no plan to it. She simply laid her harmonica on the trestle, leaped to her feet, hissed a breath, and jumped. She hit the water feet first. A mud hole beneath her opened up and a decayed, gassy mass of spatterdock roots, rising from its bottom, closed around her legs and then her waist. Astonished and repulsed, she threshed her legs and this motion seemed to widen and deepen the hole. Cooler water rushed against her feet. Dazed and suspended for a second she looked up to see Lornie leaning from the trestle watching and in her expression there was written nothing, nothing.

"You little kink!" shrieked Lydia. "I might be drowning for all you know! Don't you care? Aren't you even going to ask me not to?"

Lornie turned away and thunder in the far-off clouds pealed.

With her right leg Lydia pushed the roots away from her left one and in a minute was free of her mess. She got out of the hole and the pond and the beginning rain washed her clean.

seven

◇

For seven or eight days, or maybe it was twelve, she did not see Billy Frank. On the way in and out of the neighborhood with Lornie in tow she trotted past his house with her head held high and her back held stiff. If Rucelle lurked at one of the windows she got treated to five or six blasts of Lydia's harmonica.

Through Coochie Pepper she learned that Billy Frank did odd jobs for Mr. Dragoo at the Queen Theater every day after Bible school and when that was finished he was required to go straight home and stay there. In her head Lydia saw him chained to a post in one of the Blues' back rooms with a gag in his mouth. Coochie said Tom Ben would know where there was a cat to be had for nothing and would bring it to Lornie.

Those were queer days, some with peace. When Lydia sat with Lornie at the worktable in the classroom sewing buttons on cards, painting faces on hard-boiled eggs, and stringing macaroni necklaces, then she had peace. She would switch herself around and place herself in the role of Lornie and allow her mind to be occupied with only the simplest things. She slipped macaroni tubes on her strings, counting as Lornie counted —One, two, three, four, five, eleven, sixteen, eight, twelve. And took long times deciding whether her egg should have a red mouth or a purple one and should it grin or cry. Those hours were peaceful. There were no mysteries to be solved, nothing to be wondered about. In order to wonder about something you first have to notice it.

Lydia, as Lornie, smeared her face with Muzz's face cream. She hung macaroni necklaces around her neck and didn't notice they looked like dirty little bones. Sometimes she ate them. It was so hard to keep her mind off the things in Lydia's world. She forced her mind away from them and sat with her head on her shoulder, drowsing. When Lornie grunted she grunted. For what reason? No reason. There was no reason for Lornie herself. She was nothingness. Why then try to make reason come from her? Why try to create a reason for her?

Because, thought Lydia, as the thought of their father came stealing into her mind with a hated memory, because I want to make it change. I want him to come back and see it changed and be sorry he didn't do it. I want everybody to see and be sorry. I want. I want.

On days when sitting in the classroom with Lornie became too much for the nerves Lydia took Lornie to the railroad trestle and conducted her school there. During this season it would rain at dawn and then the sun would come out a while and then it would rain again. The daily showerfalls brought the water level of Froggy Pond up about a foot and one day a surprising thing happened. A little, floating islet, crowned with roots and lily pads and black mud, rose from its center.

Lydia and Lornie were on one of the banks of the pond when this happened. They were playing store using palmetto fronds for their counter and real money for money—pennies, nickels, and dimes. Nothing cost over a quarter but Lornie was a cheapskate. She refused to pay over three pennies for ten jelly beans and couldn't understand why it was impossible for Lydia to allow her to buy only half of a nickel sweet potato. For the fourth time Lydia explained. "Lornie, nobody can go to a store and buy only half of a sweet potato. They got to take the whole thing or nothing. That's the way it is. Now, do you want this sweet potato for five of your pennies or one of your nickels or don't you?"

"Harf," said Lornie.

"Lornie, I just told you I can't sell you half. You either got to take the whole thing or nothing. Do you want it?"

"Yer. Harf."

"No! I can't sell you half!"

"Harf."

"Lornie, play like for a minute this is a real store and I'm a real storekeeper. You're a mama and you've got a little kid at home. He's hungry and he wants a sweet potato. He's waiting for you to bring him one. A whole one. You're a poor lady now, don't forget. All you've got between you and starvation is this little bit of money so you've got to be smart and not waste a penny of it."

"The little kid is waiting for a sweet potato," said Lornie with such lucidness and cunning that Lydia jumped. Her hand, holding the sweet potato, actually shook and she thought, Aha, now we are getting someplace. "Yes," she said. "So now then it wouldn't be smart for you just to buy half of this because the storekeeper would have to charge you three cents for it. Let me explain that again. A nickel is five cents. Five of these pennies or one of these. This is a nickel and it's the same as the five pennies but let's play like you want to pay me with the pennies. If I divide them up, put two over here on your side and two over here on my side there's one left over. You can't divide up a nickel in half. Somebody's got to take one penny more or somebody's got to take one penny less. You can't chop a penny in two. See? And when you go to a store and only buy half of something the storekeeper always takes the extra penny. That's business. But even if he wanted your extra penny he wouldn't cut up his sweet potato.

Nobody'd want to buy the other half because as soon as you cut sweet potatoes they start to turn black. Now let's start over. Here are all your pennies and here's the sweet potato. I will sell it to you for a nickel. Five pennies. Pay me."

With her thumb and forefinger Lornie pushed two pennies across the palmetto fronds toward Lydia.

"Harf."

"Listen," said Lydia, wanting again to hear Lornie say the whole sentence about the little kid waiting for a sweet potato. "Listen," she said, "All right, you win. I'll sell you harf. Half, I mean. You'll have to trust me till we get home though because I didn't bring a knife so I can't cut it now. Or I tell you what. I'll sell you this whole sweet potato for two pennies if you'll tell me again why you want it."

As if to judge this question seriously Lornie put her lips together, wrinkling them. Her nickel-colored gaze went past Lydia's head. "You said—"

"You want the sweet potato, Lornie. You said why once, now say why again. Why?"

"The little kid—"

"Yes. The little kid. What else? What about the little kid?"

"The little kid—"

"Yes."

"—Is—"

"Yes."

"The little kid is—"

"Yes—"

"The little kid is—"

"Sweet Jesus, say it!"

A great disturbance of feelings, showing what must be taking place inside her, whipped back and forth across Lornie's face. She shook her head, shivered, put her thumbs in her ears.

"Lornie."

"Lemme be."

"I won't. I'm your teacher and you've got to learn. Say it! You can! You did once and what you can do once you can do again. Say it. Say it! The whole thing, what the little kid is doing."

"Lemme be."

"Idiot," said Lydia, unable to hold back her disappointment. "Idiot. Okay, you can take your thumbs out of your ears now. I won't heckle you any more. I'm done trying to make you learn anything. You can't. You're an idiot."

Lornie had taken her thumbs out of her ears. Now her face was swept clean of feeling and for a long minute she sat looking at Lydia and her look conveyed no feeling at all one way or another. Then she did a queer thing. She leaned over and before Lydia could guess her intention took the flesh of Lydia's right cheek between her thumb and fingers and twisted cruelly and at the same time she screamed, "The little kid is waiting for a sweet potato! There! Lemme be! Lemme be!"

The pain in Lydia's cheek was making the tears stream from her eyes but, in the strangest way, she felt it not at all. She only felt the thrill of success. "Oh,

Lornie," she said but Lornie drew back and wouldn't look at her or let herself be touched.

It was then that the islet came rising up out of the center of Froggy Pond. Silently, with only a little ruffle of the surrounding water, an oozy, spongy nomad piece of floating land that might have escaped from another, undiscovered world, except in the swamp surrounding the town their weird appearances were common in the spring and early summer when the production of swamp gas, working in the decaying roots and vegetable matter that manufactured them, jolted them into being in lakes and other ponds. In the dusky evenings this same gas caused the pale flames of the jack-o'-lantern to glow. There was no mystery in them. Nothing to feel suspicious or alarmed about.

Sitting on her side of the make-believe counter Lydia drew her feet up and lowered her head to hang between her knees. The pain in her cheek had spread to her nose but still she felt only a great, still exultancy. She peered at the pond picturing the grassy, buoyant islet with a flag in its middle. The flag was red velvet, emblazoned with a golden profile of her head, and the gold copperplate writing beneath it proclaimed it to be the Islet of Birdsong, named after Lydia Birdsong, famous educator.

Being turned by the wind, the islet was drifting toward the other side of the pond. Lornie had stretched out on her side of the play-counter and had her eyes closed. Her legs were sprawled and one of her cheeks bulged slightly with jelly beans. She was like a squirrel, the way she carried food around in her mouth, remembering, when it pleased her, to chew and swallow it.

Lydia's harmonica was lying next to the rejected sweet potato on the palmetto fronds and she put her hand out and curled her fingers around it. She licked her front teeth and stared at the Islet of Birdsong. On the opposite side of Froggy Pond the unanchored islet had come to a rest. The wind was making patterns on the surface of the brown water and Footsie's music was in her ears. She put her hands together and raised them to her chin, unconsciously imitating an attitude of prayer. She thought, I can get to her. It's possible. I just proved it.

Way back in the swampy sphagnum bogs somebody was grubbing for worms, using a stob. The sound of a board being rubbed against a stake made the sound of giant bullfrogs. GARUMMMMMMMMMMMMPH. GARUMMMMMMMMMMMMPH. Low and throaty. Like the bass notes of a bass viol. GARUMMMMMMMMMMMMMMPH. GARUMMMMMMMMMMMMPH.

Lydia took the stub of pencil and scrap of paper from her pocket and sat with her head cocked, listening. In a minute she wrote a message to herself: *A person shouldn't be blamed for those he doesn't love.* She had trouble forming the letters. Sweat and tears were running down her face. She eyed the message and cast a quick look at Lornie, who had fallen asleep. GARUMMMMMMMMMMMMMPH, GARUMMMMMMMMMMMMMMPH, spoke the swampman's stob. She lifted the message to her mouth and began tearing it with her teeth, pulling the pieces into her mouth and swallowing them without chewing them.

The Islet of Birdsong was being rocked by the wind and an undercurrent. For a good part of that summer it did not disappear but stayed afloat in that area, drifting from one side of the pond to the other. Some bushes grew on it to a height of over five feet and in days to come Lydia and Billy Frank, with Lornie between them, would sit under these discussing the materials of life. They would enjoy their peace, Lydia most of all, though its kind would be strange to her because it was more the absence of things rather than the presence of them.

Tom Ben brought Lornie her cat one morning. He was an old, sorry-looking tramp with one crossed eye, a crippled paw, a crook in his tail, and wild ways. When Tom Ben set him down in the living room he snarled and leaped up on the back of a chair and from there to the drapes covering the windows. A mustard-colored stain, he hung spraddled, switching his tail and mewing.

"I don't understand it," said Tom Ben, shaking the drapes. "Up to now he's been meek as a lamb. Come on down from there, Slew Foot. This is no way to act. You're not makin' a good impression at all and you know you got to 'less you want me to take you over to the Humane Society."

"He looks wild to me," said Lydia. "Where'd you get him?"

"Somebody dropped him off in front of my office," replied Tom Ben. "People just drop their animals any old where when they get tired of them. I was going to take him to the Humane Society but then Coochie said you wanted a cat for Lornie. Come on, Slew Foot. Come down now, you hear me?"

"Slew Foot's a sorry name for him," said Lydia. "No wonder he won't mind you."

"Call him anything you want," said Tom Ben. "He'll answer to anything. Call him Food. He loves to eat. Here, Food. Here, Food. Come on down, Food."

Slew Foot looked down at Tom Ben and Lydia. The way he looked at Lydia, not begging, not even asking, but as though he sensed her distaste for him and was indifferent to it, surprised in her a feeling close to admiration. He was broken and beat-up. He had a long rake mark of missing fur on his back and his ribs showed through his skin, he was that scraggy. Yet he wasn't humbled; if he was scared he wasn't going to let on.

Tom Ben said, "I need a stepladder to get him down. You got one?"

"Oh, let him stay where he is," said Lydia. "He'll come down when he gets ready. And quit threatening him with the Humane Society. We'll keep him. He'll have a different name though. His name's going to be Pawchie."

After Tom Ben had gone Lydia said to the cat, "Okay now, your name's going to be Pawchie and you're going to have a new life here. You see this girl here looks like me? You're going to belong to her and she's going to love you. You savvy? I'm going to set a dish of food down here and some water and when you get hungry or thirsty you can come down. We're going to go and do our studying now. When you get tired hanging up there come down."

"Him want drink." said Lornie, shuffling back and forth in front of the windows. Pawchie's presence wasn't exciting her or stirring her curiosity.

She went to the classroom and sat at the worktable staring at the wall calendar Lydia placed in front of her. "Wher's this?"

The silver-lining belief of yesterday was not so bright today. Lydia felt as if she stood in an empty field. Its horizons were out of sight and it had no pathways. Its brown, failed color brought a picture of her father to her mind and deliberately she drew her hated love for him from the cell where she kept it locked. It was her sword. She closed her eyes and tried forcing her mind backward to that pale, misted time when she hadn't known what a calendar was. It wouldn't go. She opened her eyes and looked at Lornie and said, "It's a calendar."

Lornie let her head lie on her shoulder. "I didn' know it."

"A calendar," said Lydia, "is what everybody uses to tell what year it is. And what day and what month. Look, here's a picture of March. See how windy it is? March is the third month of the year. But let's start with the first month of the year. January is the first. Look how cold it looks. Look at the picture of it, Lornie. See the snow? And the polar bear? Then comes February. Cold too, especially up north. Washington's birthday is in February. Washington was the father of our country. And in February comes Valentine's Day. Remember we always give Muzz a valentine on Valentine's Day?"

"Yer. What the poler?"

"What?"

"What the poler?"

"What the poler? I don't know what you mean. I was telling you about Valentine's Day and. . . . Oh, I see what you mean. You mean what the polar bear. Well, a polar bear is a bear who lives at the North Pole. Now here's March again on the calendar and here's April. . . . Lornie, are you listening to me?"

"Yer," said Lornie and went into one of her periods of superactivity. She pushed the calendar to the floor, snatched a box of colored play clay toward her, delved inside and pulled out three wads of the soft, malleable stuff. She began rolling and pounding these into her version of biscuits. Under her breath she sang, "Twer wher yolleeeeee and scroooooooble. Twer wher hip hip." She pounded one of the biscuits to the thinness of a half dollar and pasted it to her forehead. "Twerrrrr wherrrrr. Hip hip." The clay fell off. She picked it from her lap and with a thumb held it to her forehead and looked at Lydia. "Sticker?"

"Oh, certainly," said Lydia and shot out of her chair. She ran to the closet, found a little sewing basket containing, among other things, a spool of gummed tape, galloped over to Lornie, yanked two short lengths of the tape from its spool, applied these crisscross to the clay half dollar, and Lornie had a forehead piece something like Egyptian princesses wear. Lydia went around to her chair and sat down. "Now," she said. "Let's get back to the calendar."

Lornie refused to look at the calendar. She was busy again with her clay biscuits.

What would happen, thought Lydia, if I stood up and screamed until my lungs gave out? Nothing. I'd get a sore throat. I'll pretend my name is Lornie Birdsong and I'm exceptional. Yerrrrrrrr. Listen: The klutch wer down the hill and craaaaaak! Then Janie she put her eye down like this and I put my eye down like this and whffffffft! And Miss King she ho ho and ha ha and heh heh and we grunder! Phloooooooo! Wher's this? It's a calendar. Polar bear. Valentine's Day. Washington's birthday. Yerrrrrrrr.

Her legs hurt. Growing pains. Her back hurt and that pain was something else. It was raining and the air in the room was cool. It was cold, like the cold air from a cave. Lydia glanced at Lornie, who was crimping the edges of her forehead ornament with a finger and thumb. Lydia reached for the box containing the clay. She snatched a hunk from the box and with her fist began pounding it. "Scrooooooooooopt, klpppppppp-ppppt, hip hip," she sang. And slapped the purple medallion to her forehead. She put her head back and reached, like a blind person, for the spool of gummed tape. She tore two short pieces from it and applied these crisscross to the forehead medallion, sticking the ends to her skin. Now she too looked like an Egyptian princess and what was wrong with that? Nothing. What was good enough for Cleopatra was certainly good enough for Lydia and Lorna Birdsong. "You see?" she said. "Now we can go to town and people'll think we're royalty. Aren't we gorgeous? Now let's make us each a wristwatch. Yours can be yellow for gold and mine can be gray for silver."

Lornie drew back in her chair, suspicion gathering in her expression. "Dern't want no watch."

"What's that?" cried Lydia. "You don't want a watch? You're twitting me! Everybody wants a watch. They're better than brains. You can tell time with them and when you're broke you can hock them for money and. . . . Oh, you don't know what hock means, do you? I forgot. Excuse me. Well, when you hock something you pawn it. Say like you've got a watch and you need some money. You take it downtown to Getman's Hock Shop and they'll lend you money on it. That's hock. I've never tried it but Billy Frank says Harley Bell, that's Rucelle's fiancé, hocks things there every time he comes to this town. Let's make us a watch."

They made two watches, one yellow and one gray. They used a rolling pin to roll the clay flat, set a small glass on it, and cut around the lip of the glass, fashioning the cases. To inscribe the numerals they used a hard pencil. For the hands they used toothpicks cut to the appropriate lengths. When all of this was finished Lydia used more of the gummed tape to attach the numbered discs to their wrists. Lornie showed pride in hers. "Purty," she said.

Lydia sat with her decorated arm resting on the worktable. The hands of her clay watch pointed to ten o'clock and she tried to imagine what it was like in other parts of the world at this hour. In Alaska the ice fields were melting and between Alaska and Russia and between the United States and Europe the salty seas were running and in all countries the fresh rivers were flowing and the creatures in these, the creatures in all parts of God's universe, were working on their purposes. Summer is the time to work on your purpose. Your blood is supposed to be thinner then and you can move faster and see things better. Lornie was a part of God's universe. Yes. Good. But what was her purpose?

Irritable with herself for having thought of the question, Lydia tried to get rid of it but it wouldn't go. It's to show us others, she thought, us normal ones. . . . It's to give us . . . . Give us what? The beginning of several orderless thoughts, fragile as dreamstuff and too big for her, drifted from her grasp. She reached out and took another hold on them. Might it be, could it be that Lornie and other people like her really were God's children? Coochie Pepper thought so. Yeah. Coochie Pepper could speak to dead people too. But there might be something. . . . Could it be so? If it was so, why? Why would God want to make exceptional people when they caused so much trouble and. . . . Oh, I don't know. Wait. God might want them to show us other normal ones things. What

things? Well, things about life. What things about life? I don't know. I can't think what I mean. I mean now, today, this minute, when I look at Lornie I think about God. I think how good he is to me because I was made normal. And I think He might want me to be somebody important. Do important things. For other people. That's what I mean. And He wants me to be sorry for people. And forgive them. Yes, forgive. And love.

The rain had stopped and exhausted with her thinking Lydia stirred. "It's stopped raining," she said to Lornie. "Let's go out. I can't stand to sit in here another minute."

Lornie smiled at her watch. "Pawchie," she said. And over Lydia some calm and peace descended. They went into the living room and found Pawchie eating from his bowl. He didn't want to go outside. Lydia picked him up and deposited him in Lornie's arms. They went outside and stood on the other side of their gate. Pawchie hung limp as an empty sack from Lornie's arms.

On her side of the street, standing on her curb, Mrs. Dragoo was examining some of her curbside shrubbery. The plants were like her children; she could never let them alone but had to be constantly at them, dosing them with bug spray and fertilizers, reshaping them with her pruning shears, having her yard man move them to sunnier locations or shadier ones. Annabelle and Elzora were on the Dragoos' porch having a tea party. A tea party at their ages. Why, they were almost old enough to get married, both of them.

Lydia sniffed and turned toward Lornie and in that instant Pawchie decided he was tired of being held. He sprang from Lornie's arms and went tearing across the street, hurtling past Mrs. Dragoo like a rocket. Between her and her porch he selected a place and began to dig with his front paws. The dirt and little pieces of grass flew and it was a harmless thing but Mrs. Dragoo screeched, "Oh no! Not in my yard you don't!" She ran toward Pawchie and stopped. He was squatted in his hole. She whirled and ran back down to the curb. "Lydia, is that your cat?"

Without moving her mouth Lydia said to Lornie, "Tell her yes."

"Yes," called Lornie.

"Then you come over here and get him," shouted Mrs. Dragoo. "I don't want him in my yard digging holes and messing."

Lydia put a faint, roving smile on her face. She said to Lornie, "You stay here. I'll go after Pawchie." She went across the street, walking in Lornie's queer, limp way and when she stood in front of Mrs. Dragoo she looked up at her. She put her hand out to touch her and Mrs. Dragoo stepped quickly backward. On her face there was written the kind of stillness you see on the faces of people gathered at the scene of some unnatural happening. It spoke to Lydia, saying, Because I cannot be certain of what dark place you came from or your strange reason for being here, you make me afraid.

She really thinks I am Lornie, thought Lydia. And thought, Lornie has people look at her like this all the time and this is how it makes her feel. Afraid herself. And lost. Bright anger flooded her but she said nothing to her neighbor, for the exceptional ones, the tricks of nature and other quirks, must always yield. Yielding has to be their kind of courage.

eight

Coochie Pepper believed her house to be sitting smack on top of a sinkhole. She said she could be all alone in the house, everything quiet, and all at once her doors and windows would start to rattle and the dishes in her cupboards jump and she would get up and put her ear to the floor and hear the underground water flowing along beneath it in the cracks under the ground, widening and deepening the cave that was surely there. She had frequent premonitions about the hole. Someday it would open up, just like that, and her house would slide in and maybe she'd go with it. If it didn't get hung up somewhere along the way her drowned and suffocated corpse would eventually find its way to the Gulf of Mexico and from there be carried out to the open sea. It might pop up alongside a fisherman's boat. Or it might just ride along on the waves until it got to Cuba or South America. Well, it might not be so bad to be buried in one of those places. At least she'd get a Christian funeral. You needn't laugh. It was no joke. Just because some thought so didn't make it so. The world has its perils and not all of them are published every day. Beneath the dirt and other covering stuff this part of the state was like a big honeycomb, just alive with underground caverns. Very shaky. What was the name for it? Lyddy, what was it your daddy called this kind of country?

Karst.

Oh yes, karst.

Coochie had come to deliver a message from Billy Frank but it was her nature to maunder and be dramatic about her doings so first she had to talk about her sinkhole. "I don't care what Tom Ben says, I know it's there. Last night it happened again. Tom Ben's gone to Kissimmee and so I was by myself, just sitting there watching television, and all at once I could feel the house move. Not much, you understand. I don't believe anybody else would've noticed it but I did. My doors and windows rattled and I got up and put my ear down to the floor and I could hear it, the water running through the cracks in the ground. It never happens when Tom Ben's home so he don't believe it. He thinks

I'm storying to him. I ask him why would I story to him about a thing like that but he just laughs."

Because you story to him and everybody about so many things, thought Lydia.

"I would never story to him about a thing as important as that," said Coochie.

Oh no? What about that time Tom Ben went to Key West to do some deep-sea fishing and you pretended to have appendicitis and got Dr. Rawlings to say he'd operate on you and the Coast Guard had to get on the radio and call Tom Ben to come home and you didn't confess you were storying till they were getting ready to wheel you into the operating room? What about that?

To Lornie, who sprawled in a chair holding an up-turned ketchup bottle to her mouth, thumping on its end, Lydia said, "For crack's sake, Lornie, you've drunk the whole bottle. You want to be sick? Go wash yourself."

"The thing about premonitions like the ones I get is they all come true," said Coochie with a wise and wistful look. "One time when Tom Ben and I were first married we had a room in a apartment house in St. Louis and I kept having a premonition that the place was going to catch fire some night and burn to the ground. Tom Ben had just got out of the army and we didn't have any money and that was the tackiest place we ever lived in. Actually it wasn't a thing but a little hall with a screen around it. It had pink paper curtains and the landlady had to crawl over our bed to get to

107

the bathroom. You ever heard of anything so peculiar?"

Wanting Coochie to keep talking about the peculiarities of people, Lydia said, "I think most everybody's peculiar in one way or another. You know that man lives next door? The one I call Footsie? I can't get it out of my mind how peculiar he is. He stays home all the time and plays the queerest music. There's one piece nearly drives me crazy. I asked him who wrote it and he said a deaf man. I don't think that's a lie; it didn't sound like one. But I don't see how anybody deaf could write a piece of music, do you?"

"Yes," replied Coochie, abstracted. "I've heard it said deaf people can hear things we can't hear and blind people can see things we can't see. But I didn't finish telling you about St. Louis. One night that place where Tom Ben and I were staying caught fire and burnt nearly to the ground. It was caused by one of the other roomers cooking on a hotplate in his room. Tom Ben was gone, of course. He's always gone when anything important happens. That's why I can't make him believe me when I say there's a sinkhole under our house. He's never home when you can feel the house move or hear the water under the floor running and he won't let me call anybody else to have them check on it either. Says he doesn't want it put in the paper if it's true because he might want to sell our house someday and us live somewhere else and who'd be crazy enough to buy a house sitting smack dab on top of a sinkhole?"

"I think one of the reasons people are so peculiar is they don't know their purpose," said Lydia. "And they're dumb oxes. A girl I know told me she thinks people like Lornie are put here to show us other normal people things about life."

"What things?" asked Coochie, giving full attention, and Lydia could see the gears in her head turning, making plans to use the materials in this confidence at some future time on somebody unsuspecting. Say like to somebody else with an exceptional child in his family. *God put this little child of yours here to show you things about life you wouldn't otherwise know about. She is closer to Him than others and is possessed of powers we don't know anything about. This kind of little child has been put here to teach us about love. And sympathy. And how to forgive. Do you happen to know Lornie Birdsong? She is the same.*

Poor Coochie, thought Lydia. So lonesome. All those funerals she goes to and that crazy sinkhole under her house. All those voices from the dead. But no, I've gone as far with you as I'm going because I don't know any more than you do and I don't want it all turned around when you talk to somebody else about it.

"I said, what things about life was your friend talking about?" asked Coochie.

"She wouldn't say," answered Lydia. "Anyway, she doesn't know. She's a dumb ox too."

Coochie's pea-green eyes reflected her disappointment. "I told your mama and daddy a long time ago what I thought about Lornie and in the end they'll see I'm right."

"What end?" asked Lydia.

"I mean," said Coochie, "Lornie's twelve now and she's not much different than she was when she was five or six. Can't anybody make her be any different because she belongs to be the way she is. Someday it will all be shown."

"She's learning," said Lydia, forgetting to keep her teaching Lornie a secret. "I'm teaching her a few things. She's learning some."

"Sugar," said Coochie. "You're just a little child yourself. You're smart. Nobody ever said you wasn't. But it takes more than smart to know about things like Lornie. You got to have lived a while before you can see how things go together. Why, there's mysteries in this world people haven't even thought about yet and them they have thought about they won't believe because they've got to have everything spelled out for them, black and white. Well, everything's not black and white."

"And she's going to learn a lot more," said Lydia, forgetting herself further. "You watch. By the end of this summer when my dad comes back he won't be able to tell the difference between us. He'll be sorry he ran out on us. I'm going to make him sorry. He doesn't know everything. Just about algebra and astronomy and stuff like that. I used to watch him try to teach Lornie things. He never went about it the way I am."

Affecting to hide the glint in her eyes Coochie put her pink scarf over her yellow hair and said she might go to the afternoon picture show at the Queen Theater.

And asked, "How do you know your daddy's coming back at the end of this summer?"

The question struck a note of sharp surprise in Lydia for by this time the return of her father had become a piece of fact in her head. He would arrive by taxi about ten o'clock one morning and she would send Lornie out to meet him. Lornie would say something intelligent to him and he'd come up the steps and then he'd stop because she, Lydia, would be standing in the doorway and he wouldn't be able to tell the difference between them. He would look and look again and Lornie would put the harmonica to her mouth and play some sweet, meaningful notes and he'd put his hands over his face and cry. It was unthinkable that this wouldn't happen. It had to.

"Why," she said to Coochie, "I just know it. That's mostly what my plan is all about."

Coochie didn't ask what plan. She took a compact and lipstick from her purse and freshened her lips and with a tissue wiped dust from the toes of her shoes. She talked about the movie currently playing at the Queen Theater and upon leaving said, "Oh, I almost forgot what I stopped by for. Harley Bell's in town; he and Rucelle are going to be married this coming Sunday so the pressure's off Billy Frank. He said for me to tell you to meet him at the trestle. That's where he is now. He said to tell you he'd wait."

Lydia, Lornie, and Pawchie went to the railroad trestle. They sat on it and Lornie peeled a hard-boiled egg and ate it, feeding bits of the yolk to Paw-chie. Billy Frank was not there and, annoyed, Lydia said, "He's like everybody else. Can't keep a promise." She put her harmonica to her mouth and blew. aWAAAAAAAAH. aWAAAAAAAAH. Some musician she was. BLAAAAAAAAT. She put her ear down to the rail of the track and listened. It told her nothing. She straightened and turned. The Islet of Birdsong, capped with green, growing things, was on the opposite shore of Froggy Pond, but as she watched, movement underneath it lifted it slightly and it moved out and began to drift toward the trestle. The wind was light, the brown water in the pond shone in the sunshine. There was a flash of white on the bobbing land-raft. There was somebody on it and he was putting up a roof, a piece of sheet, fastening the corners of it to the growing stems.

Lydia stood up. "Billy Frank! Is that you on my island?"

On the land-raft Billy Frank rose. He held a pole in his hands and started to use it as an oar. When he was within hearing distance he called, "Look, Lyddy. Look what I found. It floats. It's like a boat."

"That's my island!" she bawled. "I discovered it long ago. I even named it. It's the Islet of Birdsong. Pole in to the bank. We're coming down."

The woods and swamp all around Froggy Pond were filled with perfect early afternoon light. There were wild calls way back but on the pond, on the land-raft, there was civilization. The canopy of the bed sheet provided shade and Billy Frank had thought to bring food and at first there was the goodness of good friendship renewed.

With Pawchie on Lornie's lap and Lornie between them, Lydia and Billy Frank sat under their canopy and Billy Frank said, "Rucelle's going to get married Sunday so I'm off the hook for a while. I thought old Harley Bell was never going to get here. I saw *The Wild Mustang* eight times last week. Mr. Dragoo thinks that's the kind of movies people want to see at his theater."

"I've been so busy with Lornie I could hardly keep track of the days," said Lydia.

"One of my seahorses died," said Billy Frank. "And I sent away and got me a new map of Alaska."

"I didn't see anything wrong with the old one," murmured Lydia. The train thundered past on the trestle above them and the engineer, leaning from his cab, gaped and then blew his whistle.

Billy Frank produced a small table watermelon. He took a jackknife from his pocket and, holding the melon between his knees, plunged the blade of the knife into it, forcing the halves apart. Its unripened meat was pale; it had been picked too soon. Billy Frank stood and dumped the two halves overboard. He sat again, gazing at Lydia. " 'Member that time we almost got caught stealing watermelons?"

"Sure."

"You lost your shoe and I had to go back for it."

"Those good ol' days."

113

"And remember that time we brought a chicken and roasting ears out here and cooked our dinner?"

"Over there. No, it was farther back."

"We didn't take the entrails out of the chicken."

"We didn't know any better."

"Funny."

"What?"

"Funny we didn't know any better then."

"Well, life is sesquipedalian."

"That melon would've tasted good if it'd been ripe," said Billy Frank.

"Lornie and I had lunch," said Lydia. "But I'm a little hungry again. What else you got?"

"Just dry stuff. Here's some crackers. Cheese. Two doughnuts."

"Only two?"

"I forgot about Lornie," apologized Billy Frank. "She can have mine."

"No, give her mine. Here, Lornie. Want a doughnut?"

Lornie accepted both doughnuts without thanks, ate them, rearranged Pawchie who dozed on her lap, put her head on her shoulder, and went to sleep. The Islet of Birdsong was drifting toward the northern shore of Froggy Pond.

"I remember where that melon patch was," said Billy Frank. "You?"

"Sure," answered Lydia.

"I remember we followed the railroad tracks up

that way about a quarter mile and then we cut off to our right."

"Turn this thing around, Billy Frank, and let's go the other way awhile."

With his pole Billy Frank turned the land-raft and it started toward the southern shore of Froggy Pond. He said, "Let's go see can we find that watermelon patch again."

Lydia looked at Lornie. "No, we can't. I can't leave Lornie."

"We can take her with us," argued Billy Frank.

"No," said Lydia.

"Why not?"

"We might have to run like last time and she wouldn't understand. She can't think quick. Besides, it's wrong."

Billy Frank stretched his neck and his black eyes grew morose. "It wasn't before."

"Before was before," she said. "Now is now."

Billy Frank turned from her look and rested his eyes on Lornie. "I could hardly wait to get here today. I didn't sleep all night last night."

Secretly it pleased her to learn he had missed her but she said, "Listen, I can't help it. How can I help it? For crack's sake, what wrong with you? You always used to help me take care of her."

"I only," said Billy Frank, "wanted to go and find that watermelon patch again. You take all the pleasure out of things."

Irritated, she responded, "Why, Billy Frank Blue,

115

that's not the least bit true. Not a word of it. When have I ever taken the pleasure out of things for you? When you talk about going to Alaska to live with the Eskimos I never say I know you're not ever going to. I always say I hope you'll write me a letter when you get there and I hope you get to see the aurora borealis and get to go across the Bering Sea to Russia. Now don't I always?"

"I only said I wanted to go find that watermelon patch again," said Billy Frank.

"And I only said we can't take her with us and I can't leave her here," snapped Lydia.

"You're different," said Billy Frank, fixing her with a frank, appraising stare.

"Oh, be quiet. You're getting my nerves on edge."

"You never used to have any nerves."

"Everybody's got nerves. If they didn't they wouldn't be alive."

"You're like an old mother hen now."

"Why? Because I won't go watermelon stealing with you?"

"The way you fuss over Lornie."

"I've always fussed over Lornie."

"Not like now."

"Well, I'm the only mother she's got all day long every day except Sunday. And I love her. Don't you understand that?"

Billy Frank was looking at her as if never in his life had he laid his eyes on her before.

"And she loves me," said Lydia.

"I didn't say she didn't," said Billy Frank, showing nettle.

"I can't go watermelon stealing with you ever again," said Lydia. "I said it's wrong now and it is. For me. Because now if Lornie sees me do something she might do it. I'm trying to make her be like me now. Last summer I wasn't thinking that way but now I am." The Islet of Birdsong was turning in the wind and she, afraid of what brewed between herself and Billy Frank, stared past his head. Their friendship which had survived so much, which had doubled joy, divided grief, furnished comfort and aid, which had at times been all, was now, of a sudden, much lessened. What was the reason?

Answer: Things were different.

Where? How?

Well, for one thing, they were both older.

Older than what?

Older than yesterday.

Nobody changes in just one day.

I wasn't talking about just one day. I was talking about last week and the week before that and the week before that. Those yesterdays.

You didn't say the real reason. Just the coming and going of yesterdays is no reason.

I don't know the real reason, exactly. I think it's. . . . Well, it's Lornie.

But there's always been Lornie.

Not like now.

Do you think Billy Frank is jealous of her?

No. It's not that.

What then?

I don't know. It's so hard to say. Lornie's exceptional and because I'm her sister I have to change myself around for her but Billy Frank's no kin to her so he doesn't think he should have to do that.

Billy Frank was poling the land-raft into shore and she, sorry for her share in the friction between them but unable to say so or attempt explanation, said, "What do you think you're doing? Why are we going in? We just got here."

"I just remembered I forgot some things I had to do," said Billy Frank and seemed to take satisfaction in the see-through lie. He insisted on leaving the crackers and cheese. He was polite. He thanked her for the ride on the Islet of Birdsong. Unbelieving, she watched him jump from the raft to solid ground. "See you," he said.

And she said, "Sure. See you." She sat looking at bulrushes and last year's goldenrod; in thick clumps they crowded this shore of Froggy Pond. It's not just him, she thought. It's everybody. I shouldn't expect them to change themselves for her. And she thought, I've outgrown him. She pounded her knee with her fist.

nine

And now it was like this: Except when on Sundays Muzz was home to share the responsibility of Lornie it was as if there were just the two of them there in the house on Poe Street, and whatever was made of their days, whatever would come from them, had to be conceived and put into action by her.

There were comalike days when, during the punctual, drumming forenoon rains, all prospects were without flavor. When, in fact, her whole nature was at a standstill.

The rain made the time pass queerly. In a way it

cheated her of valuable time, valuable because the days were going and going. The end of summer was still weeks and weeks off, yet by each day summer grew older visibly. Around Froggy Pond the greenness of the plants and grasses began, ever so faintly, to take on a look of rusty brittleness. Exhausted flowers gave their petals to the gusts and in the windows of the stores in the town summer styles were being replaced with fall ones. Yet as if there were a thousand days left before her father would come she wasted whole mornings sitting in the classroom with Lornie doodling, listening to the rain, and drowsing. What had seemed a profitable way of doing things now seemed a waste and false. For Lornie was not much different now than she had been at the beginning of the summer.

Life was false and full of tricks. Friendship? Ha. There's no such thing. There are only people who pretend. So long as they can be the big cheese they're your friends. Oh yes. But just turn your ear from them for a minute and listen to somebody else. Then they act like spoiled babies. The devil with it. The devil with Billy Frank Blue. All the Blues and all the Dragoos.

The newspaper took notice of Rucelle Blue's marriage to Harley Bell. Looking at their posed photograph Lydia could take no pleasure in trying to revive her former malice toward Rucelle. Within her, without her knowledge, it had died a strange, lost death. She didn't feel like investigating the reason. All she said was "Hick," and tossed the paper aside. Rucelle Blue was a nobody, a nothing. Who in any other part of the world would ever hear of her? She was one of those people without purpose, born with a brain to follow other brains. And those she chose to follow were no bigger or better than her own.

When brains are not as big or as good as they should be, when you are dealing with a person like Lornie and you can't get through and can't give up, then you're stuck. And being stuck you think about things like failure and suffering. You suffer because you feel yourself failing. There's no answer.

Not so long ago you thought there was.

I've tried. You can't say I haven't.

You used to think it was love. The heart must touch the heart. Remember?

Sure.

Have you changed your mind?

No. I'm tired. Everybody gets tired once in a while. And there's nobody. . . . Listen here, I'm just a kid. And if the others didn't know which way then how do you expect me . . .

Quitter.

Lornie, I love you. Lornie, it's true, I swear it. Lornie, do you love me? Can you? Will you ever? Don't, then. I can live without it. I hope you can.

One day the morning rain didn't come. It was Sunday, Muzz's day off, and come the proper time the bells of the many churches in the town started to ring and the four Dragoos, dressed for Sabbath celebration, came from their house, sallied down the walk to their car parked at the curb, jumped in, and were driven away by Mr. Dragoo.

To Muzz Lydia said, "I don't care we don't go

any more. The last time was enough to last me till I'm ninety. They knew Lornie was exceptional. To her bread is bread and grape juice is grape juice. She didn't know it was for their old Communion. How'd they expect us to know she was going to sneak out and eat all their bread and drink all their old grape juice when they didn't know it themselves? They should've been watching."

The Sunday bells aroused in Lydia feelings beyond her scrutiny. Whenever she listened to them she thought she could feel the presence of a great healing spirit and pictured it curled in the sky above her house. Its mystery and power were not meant to be seen, therefore it was colorless. From its drifting, shimmering heart a voice spoke to her: *I am the resurrection and the life. Believe in Me and ye shall be saved.*

I believe in You. I know it is Your will things are the way they are. I am just too slow to understand Your will. I am evil and I deserve to go to hell. Send me there if You want to. Forgive me. Help me. Help my sister and my mother. And my father, wherever he is.

Lydia cut a picture of Jesus from an old Sunday school paper and pasted it on the window of the room she and Lornie shared. Beneath it she taped a lettered verse from the Bible's Book of John: *This is my commandment, that you love one another.* "There now," she said to Lornie. "That's Jesus. Isn't He beautiful?"

"He were ther Good Shepherd," said Lornie. "Miss King tol' Janie and me."

"Well, that is amazing," said Lydia, pleased and carefully excited. "That you should remember that, I mean. What else did Miss King tell you? Did she say Jesus said we should love one another?"

"Yer," said Lornie, pulling open the drawer where the macaroni necklaces were kept. They all looked alike but she took a long time to select two. Around her neck they looked like strings of little dirty bones. They were her possessions and she loved them. She stood in front of the mirror holding them up to the level of her eyes as if they were jewels.

"It's Sunday," said Lydia, sitting on the foot of her bed. "Hear the church bells?"

Lornie began to prowl, leaning to peer under the beds and other furniture. "Pawchie? Pawchie?"

"Don't worry about Pawchie," said Lydia. "He's around here someplace. Listen to the church bells. Don't they make a pretty sound?"

"Yer."

"But you aren't listening to them. Listen to them. Don't they make you think about God? How big He is?"

"Yer."

"He is our heavenly Father," said Lydia, for the sun beyond the windows was dazzling and Footsie's music was coming from his house and above it there was a long, white puff of shining whiteness.

Pawchie came out from under one of the beds and Lornie grabbed him and held him to her chest. And then said a strange thing. From her own mysterious reality which chained her to the age of five or six she spoke with the simple directness of that age saying, "Father didn' want me." And laughed.

Jolted and rushing to clear the confusion, Lydia said, "Lornie, I was talking about our *heavenly* Father. God. He wants you. He wants everybody." Appalled, she laid fingers on her temples. She was making it worse, pointing out the difference between their heavenly Father and their earthly one so clumsily.

"I know God," said Lornie. "Miss King she tol' Janie and me. I know God an' I know my daddy. He didn't want me. I know." The bells stopped ringing and the great, hovering spirit above Footsie's house slinked away and Lornie, clutching Pawchie, ran through the house. "Twer ler, ding dong, twer ler hip hip." The side door banged.

Lydia ran after her, out the door and across the patio and down the steps. Too late she reached the low, dense growth of ligustrum and azalea by the back fence. Lornie went in, the foliage closed over and around her, and at last Lydia saw only the dark soles of her feet.

For the longest time Lydia stayed where she was, crouched in the long, spiny grass, staring at the gray, half-hidden shape of Lornie. The sun burned the back of her neck and she felt the beating of her heart and the pulsing of her blood. There was a big and awful meaning to this hour. To know when somebody doesn't want you, that takes intelligence. So. So Lornie had some intelligence and she had a soul of some sort. Sweet

Jesus and hallelujah. But how awful, how awful for her to realize their father hadn't wanted her.

On her hands and knees Lydia moved up closer to the bushes. God would forgive her her lie. In her ears it had a truthful ring. "Lornie, it's not true Daddy didn't want you. That's not why he went away."

"Go 'way," said Lornie. "Lemme 'lone."

"Lornie, it's Muzz's day off. She works hard for you, for us, all week. It's Sunday and she wants us all to be together. She's making us apple pie for our dinner and afterward we're all going to go for a ride. Be nice. You can act ugly tomorrow if you want to but today be nice."

"You ol' ugly. Ol' ugly. I hate you."

"Okay, if that's the way you feel about it. Stay in there and let the ants eat you up and see who cares. I'm going now."

"Go. Ugly. Ugly."

The nice Sunday had turned homely. She wandered up and down the yard counting the nails in the board fence between her house and Footsie's. When she got to one hundred and Lornie still hadn't come from the bushes she climbed the fence and sat on it with her knees pulled up to her chin. Footsie's music was going and she could see him moving around in his house, waving his arms. What was he doing? What kind of game was this he pretended? He had a stick in his right hand and every once in a while jabbed the air with it. Oh, he was keeping time with the music, directing the recorded orchestra. He leaped and whirled and jumped up and down. He went past a window, running, and for a second his wild eyes met hers. She threw up her arms and grinned. In a minute the music stopped and then he came outside. He still had the stick in his hand and he walked toward her.

She lowered her legs. She, who had never been able to stand skimpy relationships, said, "Hiya, Footsie. Happy Sunday." She wanted to hear him say something important about his experiences in the Panama Canal Zone. Probably he had been a missionary down there and not connected with the army at all. If he had been a missionary that might account for his look of suffering and yearning. In all the pictures she'd ever seen of those people that's the way they had looked, as if they were starving for something they'd never tasted.

Footsie stood three feet from her, looking up at her and tapping the palm of his hand with his stick. "It's not nice to spy on people," he said. "Why are you so curious about me? Why are you always watching me?"

"I'm waiting for my sister to come out of the bushes," explained Lydia. "She's mad at me. I wasn't spying on you. I was just sitting here looking around and listening to your music. You want to know something about me? When I hear that music of yours I think I can do anything."

"Good," said Footsie. And said, "I should go in. I don't like all this sun." He moved back a foot and then sideways, parting white daisies with his stick. He didn't go. His question swung a door wide. "Why is your sister angry with you?"

Lydia put her hands on her knees and leaned forward, licking her front teeth. Footsie didn't look starved one bit now, like a missionary, and he didn't look like a soldier who had lived in the Panama Canal Zone either. He looked like at some time or another in his life he had been a farmer. Probably in Texas. A widower. Now his wife was dead and his children all grown and gone away but at Christmas they came and brought him bedroom shoes and neckties.

Of a sudden Lydia wanted Footsie to regard her as an intimate friend, wanted him to be somebody she could air her complaints to and a person she could discuss weighty affairs with. She said, "Ha. Who knows what makes exceptional people mad with anybody? I surely don't. Nobody can understand them. We've had Lornie to all kinds of doctors and they don't know any more'n I do how to straighten out her kinks. Sometimes I think if we could live on a farm that'd help."

"I don't know anything about that kind of life," said Footsie.

"You weren't a farmer before you moved here?"

"No."

Feeling as if a present had been offered and then snatched away, Lydia scowled and puckered her forehead but then cleared her face. It didn't matter. Missionaries were just as good as farmers. In some ways they were better. They had to be educated. Quick with their wits too. She said, "Well, I just had that version of you a minute ago. I didn't have time to work it out in my mind and see where I was wrong. When you were a missionary in the Panama Canal Zone was your life ever in danger?"

"No," said Footsie, "it wasn't. I was never in the Panama Canal Zone. I was never a missionary."

Feeling tricked, Lydia gave her neighbor a long look and then turned her head to gaze at the azalea bushes were Lornie remained hidden. Out of the corner of her eye she watched Footsie pluck a daisy. She said, "Well, I guess my sister's going to stay in those bushes all day. I guess I'll go."

"Look here," said Footsie. "I was a dentist until a year ago. Now I write whodunits. Does that square me with you?"

"You didn't have to tell me," said Lydia and was surprised to hear the huffiness in her tone. "I wasn't that curious. I could've lived a million years without knowing that."

"My name is Roscoe Danner," said Footsie.

"I'll bet."

"Why do you say that?"

"I dunno. It sounds like you made that name up just now."

"I didn't. It's the one my father and mother gave me. You ever read any whodunits?"

"No, I never heard of any whodunits. What are they? Never mind, I don't want to know."

"Whodunits," said Roscoe, "are crime and mystery stories. The good ones don't tell you 'who done it' until the last page. That's why they're called whodunits. I am pleased to say I write good ones."

Lydia observed her neighbor and decided he was being genuine. It excited her that he was involved in such an unusual occupation but she wasn't quite ready to let him know it. She said, "Well, life is sesquipedalian and what's poison to one man is another guy's lyric. That's what my dad always used to say. Personally I couldn't waste my time reading such stuff or writing it either. I've got more important business to mind. I'll bet they're not so much. I'll bet I could write a whodunit. It'd be a good one. Nobody would ever be able to figure out who done it. It'd be about the biggest mystery of them all.

"And what's that?" asked Roscoe Danner.

"The purpose of people," said Lydia. "I don't think anybody knows their purpose. I see them walking around. I've been watching them and I'll bet half of them don't even know what they're here for." Lydia licked her front teeth and with her thumb gave her hair sprout a flick. There. Let the dentist and whodunit writer figure that one out. She let her head fall back and smiled at the homely Sunday sky. Tomorrow the Monday would come, yer. *Twer wher yolleeeeee and scroooooooble. Twer wher hip hip. How many minutes in an hour? I dunno. How many hours in a day? I dunno. How many days in a week? Dunno. I wanna drink.*

As if he would smell out the meaning of her puzzler Roscoe Danner came close to the fence. His bald, vanilla-colored head shone like a knob of glass in the sun and he looked at her as if she was a discovery. He said "Well, I'm not a student of philosophy."

"Me neither," said Lydia.

"I don't pretend to know any more than the next one the reason for our being here."

"Me either. I don't know. Nobody knows. I asked my dad. He didn't know. I asked my mother. She doesn't know. I asked my teacher. She didn't know. Nobody knows."

"But I've been around some."

"So have I," said Lydia.

"And I've observed a few serious things."

"Hoo-boy."

"When I was a dentist I wasn't the kind you know. I worked in a prison for men."

"Isn't that funny," said Lydia, looking across to his house. "Your house looks a little bit like one, that's what I've always thought. Of course I've never seen a real prison, only pictures of them."

"Prisons are about the unfunniest places you ever saw," said Roscoe. "But I don't regret the experience of having worked in one. I was privileged to be able to do it."

"Privileged," said Lydia and the way she felt about crooks came scornfully rushing. "I don't see why. I don't feel one bit sorry for robbers and murderers. I think they should all be drowned or electrocuted. They know what they're doing when they're robbing people and murdering them."

"Not everybody in prison belongs there," argued Roscoe. "Some of them are merely misfortunate. The reason I felt privileged when I worked with them was because they made my life meaningful. There was one in particular—"

"He shouldn't have killed his mother-in-law!" said Lydia. "She wanted to be alive too. Even if she was an old hag that sat round filthy all the time and jawed at him for being out of a job she still loved her grandkids and liked to get all dressed up on Sundays and take them to church. Even if he was wacks and had a fireball fit every Friday I think now he should have to pay." In the agitation of trying to put her point across Lydia leaned so far forward she almost fell from the fence. "I hate him. I don't feel one bit sorry for him and I wouldn't feel privileged to do anything for him either. He knew what he was doing when he buried his mother-in-law in the garden."

"He didn't bury his mother-in-law in the garden," said Roscoe. "He was in prison because he had no place to go. His family didn't want him so one night he took a crowbar and went to a public telephone booth and pried the phone off the wall and put all the money from it in his pocket and then sat down and waited for the police."

"He must not have been right in his head," observed Lydia.

"The first time I saw him," said Roscow, "his teeth were a mess. I got to know him probably better than anyone else in that place. I felt privileged to do things for him." Roscoe was caressing the daisy and looking at her and as she returned his look it was as if they hadn't been talking about his life in prison or murdered mothers-in-law or the telephone thief with the bad teeth or anything like that at all but something concerning her and only her.

"I have to get in out of this sun now," said Roscoe.

And Lydia said, "Yes. It's not good for me either." But continued to sit on the fence letting the sun brown and cook her. Intending to write herself a message she took a scrap of paper and a stub of pencil from her pocket but found the thought running through her head like a strip of film too lengthy for writing. In cherry-red letters it had the word PURPOSE printed on it and revealed her in a white coat sitting behind a desk and there were piles of books around her in all languages. They were about exceptional people and she could read them all; she had written twelve of them herself. This place was a school and she was a doctor and a teacher too and she was in charge and all her pupils were misfortunates. Some couldn't be understood by anybody but her. One was a young prince from Tibet. In the front of her school there was a silver statue of herself holding a lighted torch. A sign on it said, BRING ME YOUR CHILDREN, THOSE WHO KNOW NOT THE WAY. ANGELS COULD DO NO MORE FOR THEM THAN I.

Silly. A silly dream.

Preceded by lamb stew and vegetables the dinner apple pie was delicious and during the ride into the country Lydia sat in the back seat alone. Muzz stopped the car on a dirt road and the three of them got out and pulled grass and went up close to a fence and fed the grass to a cow. After the ride they went to see an animal movie and then, home again, ate the rest of the stew and pie.

While Muzz ironed uniforms Lydia washed the supper dishes. Lornie wanted to watch television and promised not to sit too close but when Lydia went to the living room she found her parked only a foot from it. "I told you a hundred times not to sit so close," she said. "You want to go blind?"

"Ther man in ther can see me," said Lornie. Her smile was a garland.

"The man in there can't see you, Lornie. I told you that two thousand times."

"He put his eye down like this—"

"Oh, stop. My nerves are killing me. Can't you see my nerves are killing me?"

"And he smooooooooooooked."

"Stop it, I told you! That man in that box cannot see you! He's on television! He can't see anybody!"

"And he merrrrrrrrrrkt."

Lydia yanked a cushion from a chair and turned it. She ran around the room turning all the chair cushions, beating on them with her fists though they weren't dusty. When this was done she felt better and said to Lornie. "Come on, let's go outside. I'll play you a tune on my harmonica."

They sat on the porch steps and soon it was the

time of sundown. The western sky was lighted orange and was quite a spectacle but Lornie sat unwatching, uncurious.

Lydia took her harmonica from her pocket and raised it to her lips. aWAAAAAAH. aWAAAAAAH. Like the moaning of lovesick cats. Rucelle Blue Bell and Mrs. Dragoo were coming up the street. Rucelle was carrying a hatbox. aWAAAAAAH. aWAAAAA-AH. Mrs. Dragoo put her fingers in her ears and Rucelle cast a look in the direction of the Birdsongs' house. They turned into the Dragoos' house, mounted the steps, and disappeared.

"Almost anybody can play a harmonica," said Lydia. "You want to try it? Here, you try it. Hold it like this, see, and blow. Blow. It's not hard."

Lornie held the harmonica delicately, as if it would break, and as if she would discover secrets inside them she peered into its little cells. A drifting whiff of wind shook her hair sprout. She had painted her lips with one of Muzz's red lipsticks and spread a scented oil on her neck and face. "Miss King," she said. "Miss King she play the music to Janie and me."

"Go ahead," urged Lydia. "I want you to learn how to play it. Listen, Daddy's coming home pretty soon and you know what I thought we might do? When we see him coming? I thought you might play him a little tune and then he wouldn't know the difference between us and wouldn't that be funny? He'd laugh, it'd be so funny. Go ahead. Try it. It doesn't make any difference if you make a mistake the first time. I was awful when I was learning. To be honest with you, I still am, ha, ha. Listen here, a long time back I think things got divided between us and you can do things I can't do only better and we don't know it yet. That's why I think you can play the harmonica, and better than me." The idea, born with her words, was big and hit her with a force that made her press her fingers to her temples. It couldn't be true. Could it? The thought slipped away from her. She dropped her hands. "Just try it," she said, so tired of a sudden. "For me." And so as not to embarrass Lornie she turned her head away, waiting. The sunset was almost finished, one last flare away and then calmness, a long stretch of calmness and then the sky began to darken and there was the faint appearance of a new moon.

So she waited like that not really expecting Lornie to do anything about the harmonica. From time to time she sighed and spoke automatically. "Blow. Even if it's a mistake, blow." Out of the corner of her eye she watched the dingy shape of Lornie's feet, the toes curled slightly under like an infant's in sleep. She smelled the messy child-smell of Lornie, a little salty, a little fruity, sweat and dirt and the scent of her filched cosmetics mixed.

Lydia drew her knees to her chin and waited, feeling fragile, feeling herself insufficient and forsaken. She sniffed a tear. A streamer of cloud vapor hid the lambent moon for a second.

Starshine made the moon white and there was a silence in the air as before a happening of some kind.

And then, the sounds Lornie could make come from the harmonica came. Not music, it couldn't be called that. A little jangling of notes, a little piece of language coming from the invisible world, the one where Lornie resided most of the time. They went past Lydia's shoulder and out into the night. They were pure and original. No one had ever played them before for they were Lornie's own song and in it was her spirit, mystical as a dream, a little affectionate conversation between her and the unknown, tender and hope-breathing.

In a bright shiver Lydia turned and gazed at her dusk-colored twin. In a voice struck blank she said, "What's this?"

"Yer," said Lornie without triumph or anything.

Lydia leaned to her. "Lornie, who taught you how to do that?"

"I didn' know," murmured Lornie rattling her macaroni necklaces.

"Was it Miss King?"

"Ner."

"You said she played the music to you and Janie. What music? Did she have a harmonica? Did she have one of these things?"

"Shoooooost," said Lornie.

"Lornie, what did you hear in your head just now? When you were playing that music. Where were you?" Lydia sat close to her sister and took one of her hands between her own two. There was the warm, sooty air between them and Lornie's oiled face gleamed as one seen in a buoyant dream. "Lornie?"

And Lornie began to talk, her voice rising and falling, nailing Lydia to the step, taking her to a place where there was life but without Lydia. Or Dad or Muzz. "I wer and Miss King. And Janie. We had the strawberry. Cold. And Janie she say ther the Good Shepherd. Hello, hello. And the Good Shepherd he play the music."

"The Good Shepherd was Jesus," said Lydia.

"Yer. I know. Jesus. He love me. And Janie. And Pawchie. And Miss King."

Still clutching Lornie's hand Lydia had drawn back. "Yes. Do you love Him?"

"Yer."

"And Janie?"

"Yer."

"And Miss King?"

"Yer."

"And Pawchie?"

"Yer."

"And Muzz?"

"Yer, yer," said Lornie in the softest voice and as if she anticipated the next question withdrew her hand from Lydia's and carried it to her mouth, laying it across her lips. Her shining eyes knew secrets.

The maudlin question came out of Lydia's mouth. "And Daddy? And me? What about me? Lornie, do you love me?"

Lornie twisted away and stood up. "The banana. The boat. The book. The bicycle."

Lydia let her breath out. In a minute she said,

"Oh, for crack's sake, I *have* to teach you those things. And I have to holler at you while I'm doing it otherwise you wouldn't pay attention. If you can't love me for it you should at least thank me."

Lornie made a cunning observation. "It's dark thirty," she said and jumped from the porch to the grass. Pawchie sprang up out of its tallest blades and she scooped him up and ran around the corner of the house. "Twer yer. Yolleeeeee! Hip, hip!"

A light had come on in Roscoe's house; he was playing his music. Lydia went out to her gate and leaned against it, listening. It was good. It entered her through her bones at their sharp points, her elbows and knee joints and shoulder blades. She forgot her fatigue. She had been brought unto a shelter of some kind.

ten

Shortly after Rucelle became his bride Harley Bell bought a car. It was an olive-colored convertible with white sidewall tires and fancy grillwork and at least once a day Harley and Rucelle drove up Poe Street to the Dragoos' house. Sometimes Billy Frank was a passenger and would cast a glance in the direction of the Birdsongs' house but in such a way as to make any observer think the turning of his head was an unconscious thing and his mind a million miles away. The newlyweds and the Dragoos were thicker than thieves. Coochie Pepper said the Dragoos gave Harley and Rucelle a cut-glass punch bowl and six matching cups for a wedding gift and all the members of the two families were going to spend a weekend at a holiday beach before Harley had to go back to navy duty.

"That's wonderful," said Lydia. "I like to hear about all these doings." To Lornie she said, "Don't eat that clay, baby. It might make you sick. Make Lyddy something. Make me a pig or a dog."

Coochie made a canny observation. "She's grown this summer."

"She eats," said Lydia.

"But you haven't," said Coochie. "Now Lornie is heavier than you."

Lydia jumped up from the worktable and went to the dresser. Its attached mirror was adjustable and she tilted it downward so as to observe the reflection of her whole image. "No," she said. "We still look the same. We've got to."

"Why?" asked Coochie.

"Because," said Lydia, but wouldn't complete the reason and let her neck droop and slumped her spine and was gratified and relieved to note the appearance of her stomach, a slight swelling between where her ribs left off and her belt line. She didn't feel like discussing anything heavy with Coochie.

"Sugarbun," said Coochie. "I was talking with your mother last night."

"So was I," said Lydia.

"You know she hasn't heard one word from your daddy since he left."

"He always hated to write letters," said Lydia.

"He can still talk," said Coochie. "At least as far as we know. So he could phone."

"He doesn't like to talk on the phone," said Lydia.

"You still looking for him to pop in here any minute?" asked Coochie.

"He'll be back," said Lydia. "Even if it's just for one hour he'll be back."

"Sugarbun, I don't know how you can know that. You can't. And its worrying your mother, the way you're thinking."

"She doesn't know how I think," said Lydia quickly. "Not about most things. I don't tell her."

"She's your mother," said Coochie. "You let things drop. She knows things about you you don't ever dream of."

He'll be back, said Lydia to somebody. And you know what I'm going to say to him when he gets here? I'm going to say, Sir, answer a puzzle for me. How come you can know all about stuff like Orion and light years and how to work a slide rule but you can't know your own child? And I'm going to say to him, Quit never did do anything. It's like can't.

"Someday," said Coochie, "when you're a mother yourself, you'll understand that."

Maybe. If I ever get to be a mother. There are other things.

Coochie tackled another subject. "I think the Dragoos and the Blues might have gone to the beach last night or early this morning. Both their houses are shut up and all their cars are gone. Did Billy Frank tell you they were all going to take off today, Lyddy?"

"Billy Frank didn't tell me that or anything else," said Lydia. "That big jealous baby isn't speaking to me now."

Coochie was on her way to a funeral and as soon as she had gone Lydia went to her front door and stood in it examining the Dragoos' house. Then she went to the telephone and dialed first their number and then the Blues', intending, if anyone answered, to say she had the wrong number. No one answered. They've all gone to the beach, she thought, and went back to the classroom and Lornie.

"Today," she said to Lornie, "would be a good day for you to start learning how to open our gate the way I do. How does that idea hit you?"

Squatted on the floor beside the worktable Lornie was dropping dried beans into a bottle and counting. "One, two, three, four, five, six, eight, seven, nine, ten."

"You're getting better at your numbers," said Lydia. "Except next time remember seven comes after six."

"Wha?" said Lornie, staring at the beans.

"I said seven comes after six. You said six, eight, seven and you should have said six, seven, eight."

"Six, seven, eight," said Lornie and in a motion of sudden violence upended the jar and all the beans spilled out on the floor.

Lydia said, "All right, pick them up, Lornie."

"You," said Lornie with a vehement scowl and crept among the beans, taking care not to touch them.

"Lornie, you spilled those beans on purpose and now you're supposed to pick them up!"

"Hush," said Lornie, sitting in a corner. "Lemme 'lone." Nothing promised or threatened could induce her to pick up the beans. Finally Lydia crawled around picking them up herself, plunking each into the bottle separately, word-lashing Lornie with each plunk. "You should be ashamed of yourself. It isn't just these beans I'm talking about either, it's everything. I do everything for you. I feed you and help you put on your clothes and keep you from killing yourself a hundred times a day and I teach you and take you with me everywhere I go and what do you do for me? Nothing. You only mind me when you feel like it. You never say anything nice to me or do anything for me. You won't even like me."

Lornie took four foil-wrapped chocolate kisses from her pocket, peeled them, and put all of them into her mouth at once.

"I think you might even hate me," said Lydia, rising from the floor to slam the bottle of beans down on the worktable. "Not that I care any. I don't even know why I mention it. It's nothing to me."

Lornie sucked the chocolate in her mouth and watched Lydia's face. After a minute she said, "I like Janie."

"And that's another thing," said Lydia, shaking the bean bottle, venting her anger and frustration on it.

"This Janie. That's all I ever hear out of you. Janie, Janie, Janie. Who is she? Is she real? I never saw her any of the times I went to the school with Muzz or Dad to get you. Is she somebody you made up?"

Lornie sucked her chocolate kisses. She shrugged.

"That's what I thought," said Lydia. "She's somebody you made up. But that's all right, that's nothing to me either. Come on. Let's get out to the gate if we're going. Come on, come on."

This was going to be the most significant day, yet its appearance was so common Lydia scarcely took notice of it. She led Lornie outside to the front gate and they stood inside it and Lydia said, "I'll tell you the reason I want you to learn to open this gate the way I do it on special occasions. It'll make people think you're me." The way she felt toward their father was like some living, jogging thing inside her, making her voice too loud. She softened it. "This is the way I do it. Watch me now. I come up to the gate like this, see. I get to here and I stand like this and then I bring this leg up. First I swing it a couple of times to get up my speed and if anybody important is watching I try to act like it doesn't belong to me. I talk to it. I say, 'Hiya, Pinkie. Open the gate for me, I want to go out.' Then I hook my toe underneath this little catch here. . . . Oops. . . . And push up like this and then I say, 'Thank you, Pinkie.' Just like I'd thank a person and then I put my leg back down and walk out. People who've watched me do this don't know what to think. The best part is their faces when they see me do this.

That old turtle, Mrs. Dragoo, for instance. Her trouble is, she's too normal. She couldn't open her gate with her big toe if she tried for a million years. You try it now, Lornie. You want to?"

"Ner," replied Lornie in a puzzled tone but came up close to the gate and stood there, uninterested and suffering a little.

"If you're in pain," said Lydia, "we'll go back inside and you can go to bed."

It was one of Lornie's brighter days. She said, "Pain, rain," and licked her front teeth.

"Hold it right there!" cried Lydia, excitement racing in her, for in that instant Lornie looked more like Lydia than Lydia. "Lick your teeth! Swing your leg! The other one, crazy! Your right one! That's the one you're going to open the gate with so what're you swinging your left one for? You've only got two and you've got to save one to stand on! Oh, for crack's sake, such a dumbkin. Swing your right leg, Lornie. YOUR RIGHT LEG!"

"DUMBKIN," said Lornie with her eyes gone hard and unfriendly. Holding on to the gate with her right hand she lifted her right leg and began to swing it with such enormous vitality that the gate shook.

"Now you got it!" screamed Lydia throwing her arms into the air, hopping around, whirling. "Look at it like it doesn't belong to you! Talk to it! Smile! Lick your teeth!"

"DUMBKIN!" roared Lornie and in a fast, slick motion turned so that, supported by her elbows, her body was plastered against the gate. Her right leg shot out from her body and her foot caught Lydia hard on her behind. "DUMBKIN!" she roared. "DUMBKIN YOU!" And before Lydia had recovered enough to pick herself up off the ground and dust herself off she was out of the gate and running down Poe Street. She ran all the way to the railroad trestle and Lydia, huffing and gasping, all the time twelve to fifteen yards behind her, yelled to her to stop until she could yell no more.

On the railroad trestle Lornie paused for a second to turn and look back. The railroad tracks gleamed black in the white sun. Above Froggy Pond a circle of birds spiraled and away back in the scrub, above its maples and jessamine and sand pines, other wings circled and soared and turned and swooped.

"Wait!" called Lydia to the figure on the trestle. "Lornie, don't go any farther without me!" She too had paused to catch her breath. She had run so hard and had had to breathe so fast she was light-headed now and her legs trembled in the queerest way. She watched Lornie run to the other end of the trestle, hesitate, make a decision. Watched her leave the trestle, jumping from it into tall, rough grass.

For an hour, or maybe it was two, Lornie played hide-and-seek with her, leading her through stands of sand pines, through thick growths of staggerbush and silk bay, up a little stained creek, across a dry, sandy plateau, and back again into the scrub. They went in a circle, two circles, three circles. Finally, back at the shallow little creek, Lydia sat on its bank and waited.

The bare parts of her bore bleeding scratches and welts. Green and purple spots danced in front of her eyes. Impossible to run one more step. Senseless. Impossible to stand. Was the water in the creek poison? Where was Lornie?

"Lornie! Lornie! Lorrrrnieeee, where arrrrrre you?"

So quiet. Only the wind and the sound of the gentle pulse of water in the little creek.

Not impossible to stand. Her dizzy legs carried her to the creek's edge. The water might be poison, better not to drink any of it. She walked through the creek and went up, entering the scrub again, calling, "Lornie! Lorrrrrrneeeeee?" And real fear began to possess her.

She began to run again, through dog fennel and myrtle, through twisted trees. The low branches in one of these, infested with thick swags of Spanish moss, claimed her for a second and she was forced to stop and claw herself free.

She was on a slight ridge. Ahead of her there was a sprinkling of trees in a half clearing and in this it appeared that there was a trail of some sort winding in and out. Across this trail, as she looked, there went a flash of denim blue, and with all of her breath she screamed, "Lornie! Lornie, you hold it right there! I see you! Don't take another step! I'm tired of this now and I'm mad! You wait right there for me now! Don't move! I see you!" The patch of blue on the trail in the clearing in the trees did not move.

The earth beneath her did. A slight, slow, ominous

action under her began to take place and then, directly in front of her, the earth began to crack and give way, to cave in.

Dumbfounded, as a person being shown a close and live and stunning terror, Lydia jumped sideways and collided with the spindly trunk of a young tree. Instinct made her embrace it and hang on. Her feet were still on the ground, the queerly sinking ground, and the swallow-hole being created in front of her eyes continued to widen and deepen. Bushes and grasses and dirt, even whole trees, slid downward into the inverted black funnel. There was little sound to this that she was conscious of hearing. It was as if some invisible something, holding an invisible knife to the ground, was out there running around in a circle.

This invisible something, holding the invisible knife, ran past her and the tree to which she clung swayed. She felt the ground under her feet weaken and she lifted her legs and wrapped them around the lower part of the tree. Its roots clung to their own precarious holdings. She craned and through leafage saw them exposed but still hanging on, a mass of tangled brown strings. The trunk of the tree had yielded to the upheaval and her weight and now she and it, in a desperate, horizontal, sickening position, hung over the sinkhole. She felt and smelled the cool air rising from its bottom. She heard the exclamations of falling water drops; a watery vein in the cavern beneath her had opened or was opening. The wind passed over her head.

The earth was still. It was over. Should she move? She had to move, she couldn't just hang there. She would lose consciousness and fall into the hole. The fall would kill her; the hole was at least forty feet deep. It would bury her.

There was no one. . . . There was Lornie out there. . . . Was she still standing on the trail in the clearing?

Exerting the most extreme caution Lydia forced her left hand to move downward an inch. Nothing happened. She slid her right hand downward an inch. A small commotion took place in the foliage of her tree. She thought she felt its roots pull at their moorings. She hung completely stiff and still. Mustn't move. Don't even breathe. I must move. I must breathe. I cannot hang here like this. . . . My arms. . . .

From across the gulf of the swallow-hole there came a voice calling in the most ordinary way. "Lyddy? Lyddy?"

If I answer, she thought, this tree will shake, its roots will pull loose and I will fall. And queerly, with a little shock of pleasure, she thought, She called me by my name. Lornie called me by my name and that's the first time in our whole lives that has ever happened.

And again from across the sinkhole. "Lyddy? Lyddy?"

The world had never seemed so unsolid, so treacherous, so desirable. Lydia turned her head, turned it gently, so that the sinkhole came into a clearer line with her vision. She gazed across the ruin of this phenomenon. It was a privileged sight. There were people in the world who would never see a sinkhole, had never heard of such a thing, would never hear of it. It was ugly. It was beautiful. The credit for its being did not belong to anything human. Eventually it might fill with water and become a lake. Or a pond like Froggy Pond. Dear Froggy Pond. Sweet little Islet of Birdsong. Dear Billy Frank. And Lornie, precious Lornie.

Lydia drew breath into her lungs, opened her mouth, and let out a scream so loud and harsh the boughs of her tree shook. "Lornie, go back! Don't you see the hole? You'll fall in it and be killed! Go back! Go get some help for me! I'm in a fix! Anybody! Run back to the railroad trestle! You might see somebody and if. . . . Lornie, run home! Run and tell somebody where I am! Tell them to come quick!"

The blue blur of Lornie was advancing toward the far rim of the sinkhole, moving as Lornie always moved in that queer, bent way she had. Nothing in the way she moved showed any alarm. This might be a game with her. Cannot a six-year-old mind in a twelve-year-old body comprehend the difference between a game and what is real?

Taken with a terrible judgment, probably the purest one she would ever have, Lydia thought, No, fool, she cannot. She is exceptional. *Exceptional*. She cannot understand. Will never understand the things normal people understand, what they need to understand. What if she was out here by herself? What if she had been you when this thing started? Do you think she would have had enough sense to jump to this tree? Girl, you have been spoofing yourself.

"Lornie, go back! Don't come any closer! DON'T COME ANY CLOSER!" The tears, the overwhelming tears that spoke of unspeakables, that acknowledged honesty, that recognized failure, came and she could not loosen a hand to wipe their mess away. She roared her saving insults. "DUMBKIN! IDIOT! QUIRK! KINK! DUMBKIN!"

Lornie stood on the opposite rim of the swallow-hole. She shrieked her enraged replies. "*You* dumbkin! *You* idiot! *You* kink! *You* dumbkin!" She straightened her back, whirled, and sped away. Up the trail and through the trees.

In a minute Lydia began to think of herself again. She considered her chances: If I just let go of this tree and let myself drop I'll wind up a grease spot down there. Hear the water? Stronger now, not so much dropping now, more of a gushing. There are probably limestone rocks. I'd break my back or my neck. I'd drown. Lornie will probably sit on the railroad trestle and wait for me. She might sit there till dark waiting for me. Listen, by that time I'll be dead. Listen. . . . Oh, something must happen. Something must help me.

The sky was a pale, friendly blue. The scrub, this out-of-the-world region of wilderness where hundreds, thousands of birds lived, was curiously silent. Where were all the birds? Something should be a witness to her madness, to watch either her success or failure.

She would not allow herself to look through the

leaves of her tree to see its exposed roots. How old they were, how strong, how deep they went back into the solid dirt she couldn't guess. If she could somehow turn herself around. . . . No, that wasn't the way to do it. The way to do it was to keep her position, her arms and legs clenched around the tree, her head pointing toward its top, and inch toward its roots. And when close enough, hook her foot under them. Then double herself forward and grab them with her hands. Unless something else happened first. Unless it did.

And what if, when she grabbed the roots, they gave way?

Answer: Sweet Jesus.

Go, fool.

With great stealth Lydia moved her right leg and felt again her harmonica in her pocket, pressing. She thought of Roscoe Danner and the music he always played. The wind passed over her, rustling the leaves of her tree, and then, as she began her madness, she heard the chuck-chuck calling of some bird. It reached her ears like a call from home.

eleven

The sinkhole in the scrub brought two young serious-eyed geologists down from a northern city and for several days they trotted around examining it as if they loved it while being watched by lookers from the town, among these being Billy Frank Blue and Lydia Birdsong. The geologists were safety-minded and cordoned off the area so that the gapers could not come within a hundred feet of it.

Like the survivor of an alley slugging who has been robbed of his life's savings and seeks a sympathetic ear, Lydia told her story to any and everyone who would listen: "Hoo-boy, you can't imagine what it was like. There I was hanging in that tree and it was bent way out over the hole. Way out! I had my legs clinched around it, and my arms, and every time I moved I could feel its roots give a little. It was plenty scary, I guarantee you. I thought a couple of times I was going to pass out but I knew if I did I'd fall so I just hung on and kept inching myself toward the bank. Slow, slow. I knew I shouldn't hurry; I wanted to but I didn't. I knew if I hurried I might make a mistake. In a fix like that you think of some queer things. Ho, I thought about things I thought I had forgot a long time ago. The wind came up and that made things a lot worse. I listened to the birds to keep my mind off the fact I was face to face with death. I knew my sister had forgot all about me. She's exceptional, you know. I knew if I got rescued I'd have to do it myself. I didn't want to die out here all alone. So I just kept hanging on and every minute or two I'd make myself move another inch toward the bank. That's the way I rescued myself."

After a time of this Billy Frank said, "You're wearin' it out, for crack's sake. You're wearin' me out. Next time somebody stops here and asks you what happened let me tell it. I can tell the whole thing in two minutes and it takes you an hour."

"You're jealous," said Lydia watching the geologists who were preparing to take their leave of the job. "You act like it's my fault you weren't here the day it happened. I didn't ask you to go off to the beach with your family and those old Dragoos that day. Next time I guess you'll know better."

"We've been sittin' out here for four days," said Billy Frank, "and I'm tired of it. Everybody's tired of it. There hasn't been anybody new come for two days and look, the old ones are going now. They won't be back. Let's go sit awhile on Froggy Pond."

"Tomorrow," said Lydia consulting the sun for the time. She was free now of the responsibility of Lornie which had been taken over by Coochie Pepper.

Now during the daytime while Muzz worked Coochie was a substitute mother at the Birdsongs' house and she liked to serve lunch promptly at noon. Today as soon as lunch was finished she was going to drive herself, Lornie, and Lydia to Lornie's old school for a little visit with Miss King. It had been decided that soon Lornie would again be a pupil at the school for special children and the purpose of today's visit was to acquaint her with the idea.

Coochie took them in her new car, a present from Tom Ben. It was one of those little ones that resembles a washing machine running down the road; no style to it but its manners were acceptable and Coochie drove it without fuss. Lornie sat in the passenger's front seat rattling her macaroni necklaces and Lydia rode alone in the back seat yawning. She had become afflicted with the yawns. Whenever she wasn't talking or taking part in anything active she sat around with her mouth open, half-asleep, calm about everything. So calm. For a reason or reasons beyond her abilities to dissect and recognize, peace with herself and everybody and everything had come. Her ordeal at the sinkhole had done that for her. Now she could look at Lornie and though she still wished for her and suffered pangs for her the old interior turmoil was gone.

It was like the time she had flunked math. In failure there is certainty and in certainty there is release. Her father was contained in her release. Now in her head his silence and absence were more real than before and she could not make up any more plays about him. When she went to bed at night she closed her eyes and thought of nothingness and almost at once sleep would come.

So, on this day in this summer of summers, Lydia went with Coochie Pepper and Lornie to Lornie's school and she didn't expect the time there to do anything more than bore her.

They entered the building and a girl behind a desk directed them to an office and there was Miss King who shook Coochie's hand and Lydia's and, as if she had never seen macaroni before, examined Lornie's necklaces. "Ha ha," she said. "Did you make these?"

"Yer," said Lornie.

"They're lovely," said Miss King. "Heh heh."

"Yer," said Lornie and to prove how she felt about the filthy things, took a bite out of one of them. At home in this office, she skipped around opening drawers and doors, letting them hang open or banging them shut, whichever pleased her.

To Coochie and Lydia Miss King said, "She's gained weight."

"She eats like a horse," said Lydia, yawning. Miss King was sitting behind her desk and Coochie was sitting beside it holding her scarf and gloves. Coochie began telling Miss King about how long she'd been friends with the Birdsongs and Miss King nodded and pawed through the mess of papers and books on her desk. Lornie was shuffling back and forth between the windows and desk.

"I guess," said Lydia in a loud voice to Miss King, "you heard about my ordeal out at the sinkhole."

"Yes," said Miss King, still pawing. "I phoned your mother. I want to get out and have a look at it if I ever can find a spare minute."

"It's nothing," said Lydia. "Just a big ol' hole in the ground."

Lornie left off her shuffling and was standing still with her head raised. A door was opening, ever so slowly, and Lornie turned toward it, watching. She licked her teeth and her hand went to her necklaces.

A figure stood in the door. It had mop-hair, the color of old dust, which set a stage for a young-old face. Its smile was a child's. Its eyes did not belong to childhood nor yet to the state of adults. They belonged to that yet unsettled state where Lornie and all like Lornie lived.

The figure in the door said, "Yer. Lornie."

And Lornie, running forward, said, "Yerrrrrrrr.

157

Janie." They flung their arms around each other and hugged.

Watching this, Lydia felt something of herself leave her but she could speak of this loss to no one, not even Billy Frank. After a day or two of suffering it she drew two birds on a sheet of white paper, coloring their wings and heads blue, and beneath them wrote herself a message: *I said life was sesquipedalian. I was wrong. It is longer than a foot and a half. And it is more awkward than awkward. Everybody should have to rescue themselves from a swallow-hole. Then they would know this.*

about the authors

With their first book, ELLEN GRAE, Vera and Bill Cleaver created a sensation in the world of children's books. Since then they have broken all the rules, combining daring new themes with the traditional values of humor, imagination, and fine writing, and receiving outstanding critical acclaim for doing it. "That children's books are richer by the Cleavers," says the *New York Times Book Review*, "there is no doubt." "They are creating," comments the *Horn Book*, "a new kind of fiction for young people."

Separately and then together the Cleavers moved from childhood to adulthood with ambition to write always a part of their lives. Today, after several excursions into other professions, they maintain two offices in their home in Winter Haven, Florida, and the production of fiction is their sole occupation. They have written ten books for young and "young-in-heart" people.